Praise for

"An old-fashioned book ... of cynicism, encroaching technology and intricate plotting, but imbued with a heartfelt and optimistic view of humanity—in other words, a book filled with feeling and moral values."

—*New York Times Book Review*

"This short book reaffirms A. B. Yehoshua's belief that art can help us to live with an open heart."

—*Times Literary Supplement* (London)

"It is an extraordinary book, quite unlike anything else by [Yehoshua] . . . a wonderful farewell from a great literary master, full of references to his own life and work."

—*Jewish Chronicle*

"A wise, masterfully understated work by one of Israel's towering literary figures."

—*Kirkus Reviews* (starred review)

"*The Only Daughter* is an act of gentle love, full of generosity."

—*Tuttolibri*

"We all need them—brothers and sisters and writers who speak to us as if they were our older brothers (and sisters)—A. B. Yehoshua is one."

—*La Repubblica*

"Yehoshua knows how to probe the human soul through characters who peek out from the pages at us all, as if to say, 'Hey, watch out. It's about you, too.'"

—*Doppiozero*

THE ONLY DAUGHTER

THE ONLY DAUGHTER

A Novel

A. B. Yehoshua

Translated from the Hebrew by Stuart Schoffman

HARPERVIA

An Imprint of HarperCollins *Publishers*

Originally published as *Habat Hayechida* in Israel in 2021 by Hakibbuz
Hameuchad.

FIRST HARPERCOLLINS PAPERBACK PUBLISHED IN 2025

Designed by SBI Book Arts

Library of Congress Cataloging-in-Publication Data is available upon
request.

ISBN 978-0-06-330553-3

24 25 26 27 28 LBC 5 4 3 2 1

For Sara

THE ONLY
DAUGHTER

I

The teacher doesn't hear the knock on the door. The students, captivated by the story, ignore it. This is the last lesson before the Christmas holiday, and the last of the autumn leaves flutter past the big windows. The students in the upper grades, reluctant to part from one another, congregate in the schoolyard, alongside parents who have come to pick up younger pupils. But for the teacher Emilia Gironi this is the final lesson before retirement. She won't dismiss class before further immersing the youngsters in the humanistic precepts of Edmondo De Amicis.

Only Andrea, intrigued by the boy who cares in the hospital for a dying stranger instead of going home with his recovering father, hears the knocking and cuts the story short: Teacher Emilia, he says, someone's at the door. With her copy of *Cuore* open in her hand, she walks to the door. Cicillo! She greets a graduating senior who has stepped in straight from the pages of the story to inform the teacher that the student Rachele Luzzatto should come to the principal's office with her bookbag and coat.

In the middle of the classroom a tall, pretty, curly-headed girl stands up, as if expecting urgent news. She stuffs her books and notebooks in her bag, and quietly makes her way to her coat. But the teacher, finding it hard to part from a beloved student, ties a silk ribbon around her thin wrist. Ask your father, she says, to get you a copy of *Cuore,* and finish reading this story on your own, and maybe other stories as well. But we read all of *Heart* in elementary school, grumbles Rachele, why read it again? Because you might forget, says the teacher, so you have to read and remember, and in the new year come tell me what you felt and what you thought, and if you were sad and even cried, whom did you cry over? The stranger who is ill? Or Cicillo, who refused to leave his bedside?

But how can I tell you? You won't be here anymore, you will no longer teach us. That's true, smiles the teacher, not here, not at school, but at my home. Here, this silk ribbon will remind you of me. She carefully lays a hand on her curly head, and sends the girl and the boy into the dark corridor dappled by light seeping from empty classrooms.

You don't have to show me, I know the way. But the messenger isn't ready to let go of the radiant beauty. The principal sent him to get her, and that's what he will do. Rachele studies the fair-haired boy, three years her senior. Is he really called Cicillo? No way, he laughs. Then why didn't you correct her? Because I know this teacher, I was her student, and I remember that she loves to nickname her students after characters in the stories she's teaching. Then what's your real name? Enrico. Enrico? smiles Rachele, that's the protagonist of the entire book of stories *Cuore*. Maybe, I don't remember, but even if that's his name, so what? I'm Enrico too, and I'll stay that way. We're here.

The principal is not in her office, and the devoted messenger is happy to lead Rachele to the Teachers' Room, where faculty and staff have gathered around a huge panettone cake, crowned by a cupola studded with raisins, bits of dried fruit, and sugared citrus peel, to celebrate the coming New Year. So as not to lose the girl in the crowd, Enrico holds her delicate hand and clears a path to the principal. Here's the student you asked me to bring to you, and if need be I can also take her to the rehearsal.

But Rachele will not take part in the play, and won't even sing in the choir, because her father will not allow it. Her father? Enrico is surprised. Why? The principal ignores his question, takes the girl into her office, and tells her that her grandfather's secretary called to say that Rachele should not go home but to his office, because her father and mother are delayed at the hospital in Venice.

Does the girl know the way to the office, or does she need an escort? No, she knows the way, and doesn't need an escort. Be that as it may, where's your grandfather's office? Not far from the big cathedral. But this is not enough for the principal, who asks for the name of the street. Rachele doesn't remember the name of the street but has walked there countless times. Nevertheless, the principal is wary of sending a young girl alone to the center of town, and asks for details of the route, which Rachele sketches in the air. Her right hand represents the cathedral, with three fingers raised to signify its three towers. Her left hand strolls down an alley past a pastry shop and bookstore, arriving at a square. Her grandfather's office is on a street off the piazza. There's a blue gate, which isn't the one, and likewise a gray gate, but there's a third gate, which the girl's graceful fingers push open. In an interior courtyard, tucked behind a statue of a mournful-looking woman, is a tiny elevator that Rachele is forbidden to enter alone, so she takes the stairs to the third-floor office that is not only her grandfather's but her father's as well.

The principal is duly impressed by Rachele's charming sketch, but urges her nonetheless to call home and ask the cook to come and accompany her.

"The cook?"

"The woman who cooks your meals and sometimes comes here to pick you up."

"The one who sometimes comes isn't the cook, it's Tersilla, the housekeeper."

"So let's call Tersilla."

"But Tersilla's not there, my father let her go yesterday to spend the holiday with her children and grandchildren."

"In that case, let's call the cook. What's her name?"

"Martina. But Papà sent her off too, to take the dog to the village, because at our hotel in the Dolomites, where we'll go skiing over Christmas, they won't let us bring the dog, she's a hunting dog and a bit wild."

"You keep a wild hunting dog at home?"

"Yes, and she's got a younger brother in the village."

The girl's big eyes are damp with tears as the principal listens to her, bewildered. She has no choice but to send her on her way. The sky has darkened. Do you have an umbrella or at least a hat? Rachele hates umbrellas, and didn't take her hat because Papà promised her it wouldn't rain today. The principal goes to the metal file cabinet containing student records and takes out a large, faded khaki beret, shakes off the dust and places it on Rachele's head. At least this way your curls won't get wet if your father doesn't stop the rain. Then she lifts the girl's backpack to be sure it isn't too heavy, and they say goodbye.

By now most of the teachers have dispersed, except for the music and drama teacher, who waits for Emilia Gironi to dismiss the students participating in the play. Enrico, picking at the remains of the cake, wants to know why Rachele's father won't let her be in the play. Because Rachele, the principal explains, is not Catholic like us, so her father doesn't want her to perform in a church.

"But it's not praying, it's only a play."

"That's right, a play, and we've explained this to him, but Signor Luzzatto was not convinced. 'You already destroyed enough of us Jews, so don't try to steal one of the few left over.'"

"We destroyed them?" Enrico is shocked. "Why us?"

"He meant the World War," explains the principal, regretting that she hadn't asked him to escort Rachele.

"But it wasn't us, it was the Germans," says the young man.

"We tried to explain that too," interjects the music teacher, "but he insisted that the Italians helped the Germans hunt down the Jews."

"And we must admit he's partly right," says the principal. "Our Fascists helped the Germans."

"What do you mean?" persists the messenger, smitten by the girl who had walked so gently beside him. "Her father's not Italian like us?"

"Like us, but also a little different."

"How so? What does he do?"

"Nothing special. He's a lawyer like his father, and often appears in court. All in all, it's a well-to-do family."

The principal turns to the teachers with a smile. "Can you imagine? This Jew keeps several women servants at home, not to mention a hunting dog."

"A hunting dog?" smirks the music teacher. "To hunt whom?"

"And I wanted," interrupts the drama teacher, who had been a nun in her youth but renounced her vows, "I wanted our Rachele to play the part of the Mother of God, and stand beside the altar with her infant child. The Messiah wasn't born here in Italy, but in the Holy Land. It's as if her curls, and olive skin, have been sent to us from there."

As Rachele exits the schoolyard gate, she is quick to remove the beret, but a constant drizzle compels her to put it back on. Yes, indeed—she recalls with a smile what the principal said—Papà can't stop the rain today, or maybe in watery Venice a drizzle doesn't count as rain. She's curious to know how she looks in this weird beret, but if she goes back inside, to check the mirror by the Teachers' Room, the principal might have second thoughts and insist she be escorted. She hopes to find another mirror elsewhere, and before turning onto Garibaldi Street she heads for the municipal cemetery where her mother's grandmother is buried, having died unaware that her granddaughter would turn out to be Jewish. With a bowed head and serious demeanor she joins a group of mourners marching solemnly among rows of crosses to a small chapel. She slips away to the ladies' room, in hopes of finding in a Christian cemetery a mirror that enables a living person to look at herself.

The curls are tucked under the weird beret, but her face is sweetly mischievous. Sure, she could wear it all the way to Grandpa. She returns to Garibaldi Street and enters a pastry shop with a Christmas tree in its window. The saleswoman, who knows Rachele by name, slices her a piece of holiday cake—a smaller sibling of the panettone from the Teachers' Room. After the golden slice is adorned, at Rachele's request, with a wreath of mascarpone, she retreats to a counter in the corner and relieves her anxiety with a pastry. Out the window she can see the towers of the cathedral in the distance, the beacon that will guide her to Grandpa. And as she winks at the mischievous reflection in the windowpane, she hears the voice of the teacher Emilia Gironi, who has come to the *pasticceria*, on this last day of her career, to compensate for her colleagues' failure to leave her even a crumb of the holiday cake in the Teachers' Room.

The student quickly ducks so the teacher won't notice

her. She has neither the strength nor the time to cry over some character in a book, because she might soon be crying over a man who won't be in any book. She hurriedly licks the cream from her lips and walks down a corridor toward the lavatory, hoping to find a rear exit from the shop. But when she pushes open the last door she finds herself in the large kitchen of the small *pasticceria*. Facing the ovens are tables with trays of rolls in various shapes and sizes, waiting to be baked, and the warm, fragrant ambience arouses a yen for something beyond the cake she just consumed.

"What are you doing here, girl?" From behind a stove darts a short man, a dwarf almost, whose baker's toque resembles the white headgear of the *hazzan* who walks through the synagogue with the Torah scroll in his arms.

"Nothing, sir, I only thought you might have a bread roll to spare." The baker, his hair and mustache white with flour, studies the girl, whose coat and boots indicate she comes from an affluent family and has no need of a spare roll. No, there are no spare rolls here, he smiles, but maybe, young lady, we can find you one that's not a spare. He opens an oven door and deftly scoops a mound of browned dough, sticks it in a paper bag and warns, let it cool down.

Gripping the hot bag, and trusting the generous man, scarcely taller than she is, but as humane as any of De Amicis's characters, Rachele asks if there happens to be an exit from the kitchen to the outside. She fears that her old teacher, sitting near the front door, will try to detain her.

"Why? You escaped from her class?"

"I didn't escape, I left. The principal told me to go to my Grandpa's office, because my parents are stuck at a hospital in Venice."

The baker gently takes hold of her hand and leads her among stoves, sacks of flour, and egg trays, to a flour-dusted flight of stairs, and from there, in a creaky freight elevator, they descend to a rear exit facing the ruins of the ancient city wall. No teacher will be lurking here—but do you know the way to your Grandpa?

She is, in fact, confused by the sharp transition from an elegant city street to the remnants of an ancient wall, yet certain that she'll find her way, if she can just spot the three towers. So she asks the baker to point her in the direction of the big cathedral.

"Which one?"

Rachele is surprised to learn that there are a number of big cathedrals in her city, and when the baker names them and she only knows that hers has three towers, the baker realizes she means the Basilica of Saint Anthony. In that case, he says, there's no need to return to Corso Garibaldi,

just keep going along the Roman wall, and about 300 me-
ters down, next to the convent of Saint Mary, if you lift
your eyes to the sky, the towers will be there. All three?
she smiles. Yes, all three, because the towers don't like
being apart. The baker's heart goes out to the young girl
wearing an army beret, resembling a lost soldier. And before they part, he recommends she eat the bread roll, to
give her energy, and she pulls it from the paper bag and
takes a bite, and though it tastes raw and hot, not fully
baked, she says it's delicious. And because the drizzle has
stopped, she takes off the beret and wraps it around the remains of the roll, shakes out her curls, and asks the baker,
as he bids her farewell, to put the beret in her backpack.

2

Now, as she advances along the wall, the river on her right, she thinks about a similar wall, not as high, with colorful posters pasted randomly, not far from the home of her other grandfather, Nonno Ernesto. Thousands of years ago, he once told her, the entire city was surrounded by a wall, which the Romans built to protect themselves. The Romans? The same ones who destroyed the Temple in Jerusalem? Yes, said her grandfather, sticking to historical truth. In Jerusalem they destroyed, in Italy they built. Where'd they disappear to? Nowhere, smiled the grandfather, a devout Catholic who had worked on the railroad as a locomotive driver. They didn't disappear, they just changed, and today in every Italian—he placed his hand on his heart—there are traces of Rome. Also in me? Rachele is shocked. There's a little bit of the Roman who destroyed Jerusalem in me too? Yes, even you are a little bit Roman, which you inherited from your mother, but don't worry, dear, the Roman in you is as nice as you are, and didn't destroy anything, he just built a wall to protect you.

She sees the strings of colored lights hanging from the wall, but no sign yet of the three towers that will show her the way. Rachele torments herself: was dodging a meeting with the elderly teacher worth giving up a lovely safe street, to inch her way alone along an ancient city wall? Except that here she's no longer alone. Cheerful girls in gray uniforms, escorted by nuns in black robes, exit the Sacred Heart school, carrying branches with colorful bells attached, and here and there, the sparkle of tin helmets signifies the Romans who ruled in Bethlehem when the Messiah was born. A tall monk in a brown robe holds high a baby's cradle, and a white dress peeks from under one girl's coat, and Rachele's heart beats faster: Is this the Mother of God? But where will the play take place and where's the altar?

She is shocked to find, among the marching girls in gray, Sabrina, her friend from the Hebrew class taught by a rabbi sent from Israel. Which means, Rachele bitterly thinks, that Sabrina's father doesn't mind if his daughter performs in a church, because he understands something her own father does not, that this is a play, not a church service.

The nuns steer the students to a stone building, large but plain, without a dome or bell tower, merging with the Roman wall. Rachele remembers what the baker told her, lifts her eyes to the sky, and there they are, the three towers of the cathedral, a little cloud trapped between them. Now that the towers have been located, they'll wait for her, so why not tag along with the girls, to have a peek at the forbidden play?

She hesitantly walks through the convent gate and enters a wide courtyard with a large Christmas tree in the middle. A young nun kneels before it and tries to free a furry dog, whose leash is tangled between the tree's trunk and branches. She pulls on the leash so hard she might strangle the dog. As Rachele draws closer it becomes clear that this is not a dog but a lamb—a lamb with a part in the play. In the play? Yes, it will be a horse in the stable where the Messiah was born, explains the nun, her brother brought it from the village and tied it to a tree, and the rope got tangled. If you keep pulling, the Jewish girl warns her, you'll choke him and there'll be no horse in your play. Let me help you carry the lamb and not pull it.

But the nun is afraid the lamb will bite her. Bite? Why would it want to bite you? Look, it won't want to bite me. With nimble fingers Rachele unties the rope and gathers the lamb to her chest, planting a kiss between its big ears to inspire trust. But the lamb is heavy, so she asks the nun to support the hind legs. Together they carefully descend the rough stone stairs leading to the underground hall of the convent. There are no statues or paintings in the hall, only giant candles blazing by an altar, beside which stands the student who has shed her coat to reveal the white dress as she prepares to give birth to a baby boy who will save the world from torment.

Someone shouts, "spread out the straw," and the Mother Superior of the convent, an elderly, white-haired, heavy-set woman, holds out her arms to receive the lamb, and clasps it to her heart as she approaches the altar. Don't slaughter it, cries the Jewish girl, suddenly realizing she needs to escape. As she passes Sabrina, she loudly says *shalom* in Hebrew, and the word empowers her to fly up the stairs, across the courtyard, and through the gate, and she lifts her gaze to confirm that the triple lighthouse has not abandoned her. The towers indeed have not budged, and await to guide her to her grandfather, and the pesky cloud that shrouded them has vanished.

3

In the maze of alleyways the towers disappear once
again, but now Rachele, knowing the name of the cathedral, is not worried. She need only utter the blessed
name to passersby and they will show her the way, sometimes in excruciating detail, but she doesn't require every
detail, just the right direction. Moreover, bells have suddenly begun to ring, drawing her to the piazza where the
cathedral stands in its full glory, exulting in festive song.

Years ago, Nonno Ernesto took Rachele to a children's celebration at the cathedral and Papà was angry with him.
But now Papà is in the hospital, and won't know that she
yearns to revisit the interior she saw in her childhood. She

carefully pushes open the heavy wooden door, then pauses. The cathedral is empty, the aroma of incense hanging in the air, afternoon sunshine dancing in the big, colorful stained-glass windows depicting ancient animals and forgotten prophets. Deep inside the church is the altar, upon it a sparkling golden chalice. Is there any wine left? For a moment she wants to take a peek, but knows that Papà will be very angry if he finds out that she went to the altar, and her father, say his friends, can get people to confess to things they haven't even done. She freezes in place, her gaze wandering across the ceiling over which the three towers rise high. Does the pinkish baby, floating up above at its mother's breast, know he will end up naked and wounded on the cross, as in the painting behind the altar, or is he an innocent babe, who believes he will manage to remain a simple Jew?

The first, muffled chord of an organ hastens her exit. For a moment she's not sure she's found the right alley, because the bookshop was taken over by a pizzeria that kept a few books on two shelves, to give added value to the pizza. But the square is the same and Grandpa's street hasn't moved. The blue gate, then the gray one, and now the gate that leads her to the courtyard, where the woman carved in stone grieves in front of the little elevator. A young man holds the door open for Rachele. Which floor, Signorina? Third floor, please, she answers, and he presses the third button, and also the second, whereupon her hand goes out to block the door. No, sorry, sir. She is not allowed to ride alone in this old elevator, not even one floor. But the young man won't pass up the company of such a beautiful girl, so he'll escort her to the third floor, then go down to the second. But why the third floor? he wonders, it's all dark, everyone's gone for the holiday. Not my Grandpa, the attorney Luzzatto. Ah, the young man says, smiling strangely, you're the granddaughter of the Jewish attorney. Exactly, the only grandchild.

The floor is dark, and the office too, because the assistants, interns, and staff left for Christmas vacation yesterday. Only Valeria, the personal secretary, was asked to stay behind. What happened to you? We thought maybe you stayed for the rehearsal after all, the janitor said the principal sent you here almost an hour ago, so what happened? Your grandfather is so proud that you know your way around. Yes, I'm sure of the way, but an elderly teacher, who won't be teaching us anymore, delayed me, to ask that I finish reading a story I missed the ending of in class, and she wants me to cry for its hero. A story? The secretary chuckles. Why cry over a story? Because it's a story from *Cuore*, a famous book that you surely know, an old book. It's not worth crying over old books, says the secretary, now let's tell Grandpa you're here, he's in a meeting, and I have to run home to cook for the holiday. You Jews already had your holiday, but ours is just beginning.

Yes, confirms Rachele, and it's not a complicated holiday, just candles and potato pancakes. But wait, what about Papà? Are they still in Venice? And why Venice, anyway? Because your grandmother arranged a meeting with her friend, the director of the hospital in Venice, who will supervise the tests personally, but let's go say hello to Grandpa, because he's worried about you.

With the pack still on her back, Rachele enters the smoke-filled conference room. Grandpa Sergio sits at the head of the table, surrounded by his "farmers," as his son calls people from the surrounding villages, who believe that a smart Jew can make difficult decisions for them.

"See," says the grandfather, rising to his feet, "I told you my granddaughter knows the way."

The heavy-set "farmers," some wearing overalls and old caps, plus an aged monk in a black robe, a large gilded cross upon his chest, politely echo the Jewish lawyer's pride in his only grandchild.

But Valeria has no time for pleasantries. She takes Rachele to her father's office at the end of the corridor and opens the blinds to let in the light. Since the office kitchenette is closed, she has nothing to offer the young visitor other than tea. No need, says Rachele, I'm not sick or hungry, on the way here I ate a slice of panettone, and a dwarf baker gave me a bun. The secretary takes a woolen blanket from the closet and lays it on the big leather couch, and parts with a kiss from the girl she has known since her birth.

But Rachele doesn't want to lie down on the sofa. She prefers to sit at her father's desk and inspect his drawers. She removes the backpack and takes out the remains of the bun. It apparently continued to bake inside the weird beret, for the original raw taste has acquired a sour sweetness. There aren't as many file folders here as in Grandpa's office, or even a tiny office like Valeria's. I take care of people, her father brags, I appear in court and argue with human beings, while your Grandpa is busy with documents. Hearing this, the grandfather would respond with a smile. Without documents there are no people.

Precise scale models of cars and motorcycles, racing cars mostly, are scattered on the few shelves in the room, along with pipes of various shapes, and on two shelves are seashells of different sizes and colors, collected on the beaches of Italy and Israel.

An ashtray, overstuffed with cigarette butts, is hidden in the top drawer beside an unopened carton of American cigarettes, purchased on a flight from abroad. The cigarettes, not the motorcycle, will kill your father in the end, the grandmother from Venice declares again and again. Given such a warning, the incriminating ashtray is concealed in the drawer. Rachele would like to throw the carton out the window, but it's raining outside and the cigarettes will be soaked instantly and no passerby could enjoy them. The young handsome rabbi from Israel taught them the law of *bal tashchit*, which forbids destroying something useful.

What's *bal*, asked Sabrina, *bal* means no, said Rachele, who has a knack for the ancient tongue. So why do people say *bal* instead of the regular word *lo*, persisted Sabrina. So you'll have something to ask and I'll have something to explain.

Because of that *bal tashchit* prohibition, Rachele shoves the carton into the innards of the leather sofa. Yes, he can always buy another carton, but at least this carton won't kill anyone until the sofa ends up at the flea market.

Angry voices from the conference room slowly subside, and after a brief silence, her Grandpa can be heard, apparently suggesting a solution. Rachele can't make out the words, but Sergio's confident tone, which sometimes calms her too, cools the tempers of the "farmers." Now the Jew leaves it to them to digest his proposed solution, and goes to his son's office. Wonderful, he joyfully greets his granddaughter seated at her father's desk, you're in exactly the right place, you'll also study law, and manage this firm when your father and I are both gone. He takes off his shoes and stretches out on the leather sofa.

"How lovely and pleasant is the vacation that the Catholics give the Jews. A long, official vacation, with no prayers, no big meals, no gifts. A holiday with no obligations."

"You're done with your farmers?"

"You also call them farmers? No, darling, they're not all farmers, one is an important monk, now selling some of his monastery's land. I left them alone on purpose, so they will feel that the proposal on the table is not mine but theirs, the one they reached on their own. When you run this office, do as I do. Put the right solution on the table, and leave the room, so they can't say the Jew forced them to sign. You understand?"

"Sort of, not really, but is this how you always do it?"

"Exactly, and you'll behave the same way in the future, but there's plenty of time, meanwhile you're starting a long vacation, and in two days you'll be going to a hotel in the mountains, to ski and have fun in the snow. Are you happy?"

"No, Grandpa, I'm not happy, I'm sad, very sad."

"What's wrong?"

"I wanted so much to be in the school play, tomorrow afternoon in the church, but Papà said I couldn't."

"He said you couldn't? Why?"

"Because the drama teacher chose me, even though I'm the youngest in the class, to play the part of the Mother of God. She thinks it is right for me because of my curls and my clear voice, and I had learned the role by heart, and then Papà interfered and warned the principal not to include me, not in the play or even in the choir."

"Not even in the choir? Why?"

"Ask him, he's your son."

"Oh, I'm so sorry, why didn't you tell me?"

"What good would it do? He usually doesn't listen to you."

"Yes, but this time I would have persuaded him. Oh, sweetheart, what a shame you didn't tell me. Honestly, would something terrible happen if you once played the Madonna and for an hour you'd be the Mother of God, it's a play, not a church service."

"Precisely, Grandpa, precisely," says Rachele excitedly. "Everyone explained that to him, the teachers, the principal, but he was stubborn, so instead of standing by the altar in a white dress tomorrow, and giving birth to the holy infant in front of all the students and their parents, I'll sit alone at home, depressed."

"Not give birth," the grandfather mutters with a smile, "just pretend, but it really is too bad you didn't tell me, I might have convinced him."

"Convince? What would you say that the teachers haven't already said?

"If I explain to him the deep reason for his opposition, he would definitely understand and change his mind."

"Deep reason? Oh, what a mistake I made not telling you. The father you gave me is hard to deal with sometimes."

Tears glisten in her big eyes.

"So from now on tell me when you have a hard time with your parents, and I will try to help. After all, you're my only grandchild, and I'm proud of you. You saw how I show off your writing in my office to everyone."

"Then tell me what you'd say exactly."

For a moment the grandfather is wary of revealing a dark secret from his past, but the desire to share his sudden insight with his darling granddaughter wins out. I would explain to him, he says, that it's not because of you that he objects to your being the Mother of God, it's because of me.

"Because of you?"

"Because he knows that during the War, to save my life, I became a priest in the church, and he's afraid that if you start visiting a church, even for just a play, you might start to like it."

"A priest? You?"

"Only during the War. When they started handing over the Jews to be murdered, your grandmother, who was about to give birth to your father, was hiding in a tiny hotel in the Dolomites, and I couldn't be with her, because everyone knew I was Jewish. I turned to my old law professor from Bologna, a devout Christian, but a man who loved me, and he lent me the name of his son, who died in his youth, and provided me with forged documents, and through a friend in the Vatican arranged for me to substitute for a priest in a small town, not far from the sea, who had recently died."

"Which town? Which sea?"

"I will never reveal the name. Or the region. Even your grandmother doesn't know, nor does your father. From the day the War ended I never went near it again."

"But how did they let you be a priest? How did you know how to do it?"

"It's not that hard, I knew Latin well, and the professor taught me the prayers and rituals, and what I had to do on holidays, and mainly showed me how to take confessions, something that serves me well as a lawyer to this day."

"And where did you live?"

"The priest's house that belonged to the church. The women would bring me food, and I had everything I needed."

"And nobody suspected that a Jew was hiding in your soul?"

"Who knows, but when I felt they were starting to suspect me, I left, disappeared. I was a priest for maybe a year and a half."

"But still, when you prayed and sang, weren't there moments when you felt that Jesus really was a bit of a god, who performed all those amazing miracles, and therefore the Madonna, his mother, really is the Mother of God?"

"What can I say, dear, your questions are not simple, which is why you'll be a good lawyer. Yes, sometimes, a little, why not, I believed in their saints out of gratitude. They saved my life, after all. If Muhammad or Buddha had saved my life, I would start believing in them too and praise them."

"Buddha? Who's that?"

"The god of the Indians and Japanese and many other nations."

"You'd pray to him too?"

"Why not, if our God was too weak to save us, why shouldn't we pray to other gods? I mean, at least make a show of prayer. But for the townspeople I led the prayers correctly and enthusiastically, and they prayed and sang with me. But my dear, don't you ever utter one word about this to anyone, especially not your grandmother, who thinks I actually intended to convert to Christianity."

Soft knocking at the door. The abbot, in his black robe, and a potbellied "farmer" stand at the office doorway. Excuse us, Signor Luzzatto, in the end we decided to accept the solution you proposed.

"A wise decision," says Grandpa, bolting from the sofa. "And you've signed it?"

"Yes, on all the pages you marked."

"Excellent. But don't forget, Father Abbot, you must obtain official permission from the Vatican."

The abbot nods, he won't forget. Wonderful, gushes Grandpa, and now, my dear friends, Lorenzo, Pietro, please, before you leave, say hello to my granddaughter, Rachele Luzzatto, who in the future will join this law firm, and run it with Riccardo when I'm no longer around.

"He should be well, Riccardo," says the abbot, his small, braided pigtail swaying on his nape, "we all pray for his health." As he places his ring-encrusted hand on Rachele's head to bless her, he notices the ancient khaki beret on the desk and picks it up.

"Where did you find this beret, Signorina?"

"The principal gave it to me today, before I left the school, because it started to rain . . ."

"Interesting." The abbot's blue eyes light up and the braid again brushes his neck. "During the War, our partisans wore berets exactly like that one."

"The partisans?"

"Yes, and at the monasteries we still keep clothes and belongings of people who hid with us during the World War and never came back to get them."

4

I n the silence that prevails after the "farmers" depart, the daylight grows weaker, and Grandpa turns on another lamp in his office, still not thinking to ask if Rachele has eaten since breakfast, and when she—hungry again, despite the cake and bun—suggests they wait for her parents in a restaurant, he resists. The rain is heavier now, the lunch hour is over in the restaurant, only leftovers will be available, and at home a meal awaits them, prepared by the cook. There's no meal, Rachele declares, Martina was sent to the village yesterday with the dog, because dogs are not allowed at the hotel. No problem, says Grandpa, your mother will cook something for you. No, Grandpa, Mamma hates to cook, and when she does cook, the food has no flavor. Come on, let's go down to the restaurant, pleads the granddaughter, almost in tears, arousing not only Grandpa's pity but his appetite, so he asks for half an hour to deal with certain matters he might forget, and then they'll go wherever she wants. But you never forget anything, grumbles Rachele, why are you afraid of forgetting today? And she suggests the pizzeria that devoured the old bookshop. Very good, Grandpa readily agrees, we'll go there, because you're an expert in finding the best food in town, and Rachele throws her arms round the neck of her Jewish grandfather, a slender man, carelessly elegant, who excels as a dancer at community events.

"When you were a priest . . ."

"Ah, I'm sorry I told you . . ."

"Okay, I promise to keep quiet, but when you were a priest, you had to feed the Christians the holy bread . . ."

"Of course, that's part of the ritual."

"But what is the holy bread exactly?"

"It's a kind of cracker, which symbolizes the body of Jesus."

"Did you maybe save a few of those holy crackers?"

"How, silly girl? It was more than fifty years ago."

"But what does this cracker taste like? I'd like to try it some time."

"It has no taste. It's dry, thin, and disappears in the mouth."

"If I were a Jewish priest, instead of tasteless crackers

I would feed my believers tiny pizzas, as long as the rabbi pronounces them kosher."

"Pizzas?" The grandfather is amused.

"Why not? If you have to eat something of God, it should at least taste good."

And she sighs and returns hungry to her father's office, turns out the light, lies down on the leather sofa, and the moment she snuggles under the blanket, it gives off the scent of her father's shaving cream, and she dozes off, missing him.

But when her mother's agitated voice echoes beyond the office wall, Rachele discovers her father sitting at his desk, leafing through a newspaper. The ashtray hidden in the drawer sits before him on the empty desktop, containing only one cigarette butt.

"Papà, you're back!" she squeals with delight.

Rachele jumps into his open arms, hugging and kissing, and he buries his head in her curls, smelling her hair, and when she tries to sit on his lap he says, what is this? You're a baby again? But she climbs onto his lap, lays her head on his chest, listening to his beating heart with her eyes closed.

"Why are you so late?"

"It took time. Venice is a city for movies, not human beings."

"And why is Mamma so upset? What is she telling Grandpa?"

"What the doctor said."

"And why is she crying?"

"Because she thinks I'm dying."

"Are you really dying?"

"Of course not."

"Don't you dare want to die."

"Why would I want to die?"

"Promise me that if you're going to die, you will die when you're very old, die at the end, die when I'll also reach the end."

"I promise."

"Because I'm still mad at you."

"Why?"

"That you didn't let me act and sing in the Christmas play. Grandpa was also very cross with you."

"Again that play? Why is it so important to you?"

"Because the drama teacher wanted me to be the Mother of God, she said I fit the part because of my clear voice and my curls. And besides, I was the first one in the class who knew the part by heart."

"The drama teacher should find herself a Catholic Mother of God," Papà declares. "There's no shortage of suitable girls."

"You're mean. You're really not okay. Sabrina's father doesn't mind at all that she sings in a Christian choir."

"How do you know?"

"I happened to see her today at the convent of Santa Maria."

"What? How'd you end up in the convent? Why'd you go in there?"

"I didn't go in, I happened to pass by, but outside there was a panicky nun who needed my help to bring a lamb to the play, because she was afraid the lamb would bite her, and I calmed her down and took the lamb into the convent for her and I saw Sabrina singing in the choir."

"A lamb for a play? The nuns have gone totally crazy."

"Why not a lamb, if they want the play to be realistic? Jesus was born in a stable, but it's hard to take a horse into a church, so why not bring a lamb?"

"I don't mind, for all I care they could bring lions. But I do mind that you're going around to monasteries and churches."

"But Sabrina's father doesn't care, even though she's also Jewish like me. And anyway, she spends all day with the nuns at Sacred Heart."

"That's because her parents have no money. They're both studying medicine, and they sent Sabrina to the nuns because the students stay at school till four in the afternoon, and get free meals."

"But they're still Jews, and they're not afraid of the nuns as you are."

"They're not afraid, because when they become doctors

they'll move to Israel, and there all the brainwashing Sabrina gets from the nuns will be erased. But you are staying in Italy, and here, there's a church or convent on every street, and the bells never stop ringing."

"But the churches are mostly empty."

"Empty? How do you know? Maybe now they're empty, but what will happen in the future? Take care of yourself, it's not hard, and in general"—he suddenly shakes free of her and sets her on her feet—"enough crying over nonsense and enough self-indulgence. There are far more serious troubles you need to prepare for."

As he puts her at a distance, she feels the tension bubbling inside him, as before an important court case, when the opposing lawyer turns out to be serious and sophisticated, but this time the adversary is inside his own brain.

Her grandfather and mother enter the room. A new fear is apparent in the mother's weary eyes while the grandfather, holding two large envelopes with x-rays, strives as always to be rational and practical. He will take the x-rays with him on his holiday in Capri. They're traveling there tomorrow, because his Carla loves to attend the Midnight Mass at the fishermen's church near the port. And while on vacation he can consult calmly with his friends, companions on holidays, well-known medical doctors, Jews and non-Jews, heads of hospital departments in Rome and Milan. With plenty of time on their hands, they'll be able to take a close look and reach the right decision, namely, whether to wait or hurry to do surgery.

"No surgery," says Papà, "there's nothing there."

"We'll get advice, we'll see what's what," says Grandpa, "we're in no hurry. But do you really think that in your condition it's wise to travel tomorrow to the snow and the cold? Doesn't it make more sense to rest at home for a few days, and then celebrate the New Year at a hotel that's closer, at one of the lakes?"

"No, *babbo*, we're going to the mountains, Paolo will take us and the motorcycle tomorrow evening."

"Paolo? Why? Even now you can't do without the motorcycle?"

"Why not take it? This might be the last time."

"Don't even say it."

"What, the evil eye?" The father laughs, picks up the old beret and waves it. "What's this rag doing on my desk?"

"It's not a rag, Papà, it's a beret the principal found for me so I wouldn't get soaked in the rain."

"And where's your hat?"

"I didn't take it, because you promised me it wouldn't rain today."

"I promised, I said, I promised, I said," mutters the father irritably, "not everything I say is holy, but anyway, why couldn't the principal find something more dignified than that rag?"

"It's not a rag," interjects the grandfather, "the abbot who was here said it was a partisan's beret from the War."

"If so," Papà opens a drawer, tossing the beret inside, "we'll save it for the next war, and in the meanwhile, liberty, freedom, vacation, and maybe a little life."

"Your mother knows about the tests?"

"Of course. It was the director of the hospital who took me from test to test, and did this not for me but for her, and he undoubtedly told her the results and what they mean, including conclusions he is still afraid to tell me personally. By the way, *babbo*, you've probably heard of the director, Salvatore Novarese, who is not only a great doctor but a man of culture. Could he also be one of Mamma's lovers?"

"Riccardo, enough! How many times have I cautioned you that I haven't the slightest interest in the lovers of my former wife. And for the love of God, watch what you say in front of your daughter."

5

The city glitters with colorful holiday lights, strung all over town. In the windows of shops, especially those selling toys or kids' clothes, dolls perched on heaps of white Styrofoam beads are meant to represent the nativity scene of two thousand years ago, in a hot village that got barely a snowflake in winter. But in this northern Italian city, a few flakes are already scouting the territory. We don't need to look for snow in the Dolomites, says Rachele, it's already heading here. But we're not looking for snow, says the father, but thick, strong ice, because Jewish skiing on Christmas is also a prayer in memory of Jesus of Nazareth. Why his memory? Mamma objects. He was born on Christmas, he didn't die on Christmas. You're right, my mistake, not in his memory but in his honor.

When the car passes the new pizzeria that swallowed the bookshop, Rachele suggests they try it. I know there's nothing in the house, and I'm starving, and all I've had since noon is a half-baked bun that a merciful midget gave me. But her father is unwilling to stop anywhere, there's no place to park, and a mob of shoppers. We can always find something at home. Yes, something cold and raw, the mother chimes in, because you sent Martina to the village too early. Right, grouses Rachele, why the burning need to send her? We could have asked Grandma's driver to take care of the dog. Don't say Grandma's driver, he has a name. Fine, Paolo can look after Diana. Paolo can't, he has a small dog at home, which Diana would destroy, but in the village she has a younger brother, and they can run through the fields together. Not only you, young lady, are entitled to a vacation, so is your dog. In any case, what can we eat? I'm hungry, really hungry. In the church, at the play rehearsal, I'm sure they supplied fantastic pizzas for everyone. Enough with that Christian play. There'll be real food at home, because this time I'll do the cooking. You of all people? says the mother, you're tired and ill. No, I have the strength, and when I want to, I can cook.

In the spacious apartment, an exquisitely renovated penthouse, the mother phones her parents with test results. Tomorrow, before setting out for the mountains, they'll stop by their house to wish them a happy New

Year, and receive the gifts that await them, but her anxiety over the medical diagnosis compels a quick update. Rachele joins the call, to ask if Nonna might have a copy of the book *Cuore*, because her teacher Emilia told her to finish reading a story started in class, and also another story, and then come and tell the teacher her impressions. *Heart*? Nonna is shocked. They still teach that nationalistic book? Why read a book that encourages children to sacrifice themselves in needless wars? Wars? gasps the granddaughter, which ones? The grandfather intervenes: don't pay attention to what Nonna says, she's the last person in the world who still doesn't know that pacifism is an empty word. I'll look for a copy of *Cuore*, and if I can't find it, we'll buy you a new one.

Papà, clad in an apron, pokes around the kitchen to check what's available, and as he contemplates the next meal, he tells his daughter to gather up all the hunting dog's toys, and the leather bone that sharpens her teeth, and put them all in her empty cradle. I miss her already, says Rachele. But she doesn't miss you, Papà responds, because soon she'll give us another litter of pups, so instead of nostalgia, what should I make, spaghetti or risotto? Make what you know how, in other words spaghetti, but a lot, because otherwise I'll be so hungry I'll gobble you up. And please make sure the spaghetti doesn't get too soft, and I'll grate the Parmesan.

Very rarely does Riccardo Luzzatto make a meal for his family, mostly he doesn't eat at home. Yet he thinks of himself as a cooking maven, and when he is captivated by a dish at a restaurant he walks into the kitchen to learn the secret. And though he listens carefully to what he is told, he doesn't take notes, and there's no way to know what he remembers when he decides to re-create the dish for his family.

Outside it's snowing heavily, and a freezing wind is blowing, but it's warm in the house, so Rachele emerges from her shower in a lightweight nightshirt, and goes to call her mother to the table, but her mother is curled up in fetal position, trying to banish the bad news from her mind. Rachele is careful not to wake her, turns out the light and closes the door, and en route to the kitchen she darkens the hallway too, so no light will restore her mother's consciousness. In the large, spotless kitchen, fragrant spaghetti, mixed with the ricotta, awaits the final touch of grated Parmesan.

"Mamma is sound asleep, you sure you want to wake her?"

No, don't wake her, she needs the sleep to get used to the fear that's consuming her. Fear of what? I don't understand, and you don't explain a thing. Later on, you'll understand it all, but now, let's eat, you said you were hungry, so I added zucchini and asparagus to the spaghetti, just so you won't eat me.

Her hunger mounting at the sight of the meal, she slurps the spaghetti quietly, her eyes misty with mute gratitude as Enrico, who held her hand in the teachers' room, flickers in her memory alongside a muddy mirror in a graveyard, a dwarf baker and the hot batter, the ride in an old elevator to a Roman wall, a chubby Mother Superior who takes a lamb from her arms and places it beside the white dress of the Mother of God.

Her fork twirls the spaghetti, again and again, but when she looks at her father, she sees that his plate is empty. Why aren't you eating? Are you waiting for Mamma to get up? No, let her sleep. But you, if you like the spaghetti, take more.

"And you, Papà?"

"Later . . ."

Now she understands that the fear that devastated the mother has gripped the father too, and has started to seep inside her as well. She puts down the fork, moves the plate, and shudders: "Please, Papà, the truth."

"The truth?" He smiles. "The truth? You really want to know? This time the truth is a bit strange."

"Why strange?"

"If you can imagine, the doctor in Venice thinks my brain may have grown slightly."

"Your brain? Why?"

"Maybe because the world has become more complicated, and to understand it the brain has to get bigger."

"Bigger? On its own?"

"Yes, on its own."

"You mean, like an appendage?"

"Bravo, an appendage, you found the right word."

"And this happens also to other fathers?"

"Sometimes. Why not, I'm not special."

"And what will they do with your appendage? Leave it? There's enough room for it?"

"That's the question, is there room for it in my head, or does it have to be removed."

"But how? The head is closed, no?"

"Everything that's closed can be opened."

"Also the head?"

"Today they can open anything."

"And if they discover that it's a good appendage, they'll leave it in you?"

"No, even if it's good they'll explain to it that the brain of Rachele's father is good enough to understand the world, so you, strange appendage, are unnecessary."

"Who's going to say that?"

"The doctor."

"And then?"

"They'll remove it."

"And then?"

"Enough . . . Bedtime."

But Rachele feels her father is deceiving her because he's afraid of scaring her. So she doesn't give up, she takes the empty plate to the sink and rinses it, and whispers as if to herself, I know what this comes from, it's all those cigarettes you smoke, your mother even said: the motorcycle won't kill your father, it's his cigarettes.

"But it's a fact, the cigarettes didn't cause the illness, that's a fact."

"Illness?" Rachele is shocked. "The appendage is an illness? What caused it? Anyway, the fact is I saw an ashtray full of cigarette butts that you hid in your desk drawer."

"They're just some old butts I didn't get around to throwing out, and I hid them because I didn't want anyone to think I smoked them all in one day."

"Why didn't you want that?"

"Because there's always someone who makes a remark, even if they have no right. By the way, was there also a sealed carton of new cigarettes? Did you come across it?"

"What's a carton?"

"The truth, Rachele, just the truth. Because my mother said that cigarettes would kill me, you decided to throw it out? The truth, and you know that I know how to get the truth out of anyone."

"Okay, maybe that's right, more or less, I tried to throw them into the courtyard, but it was raining, and I didn't want whoever found them not to be able to smoke them, our rabbi taught us about *bal tashchit*.

"What is *bal tashchit*?"

"Not to destroy or waste something useful."

"So what did you do?"

"For the time being I just hid them."

"Where?"

"In the sofa in your office. But please, don't keep smoking."

"No, I won't smoke those cigarettes, I'll leave them in the sofa."

He gets up and hugs her tightly, kisses her forehead, and says, "Enough, go to sleep. Tomorrow evening we'll go to the mountains, Paolo will drive us in Grandma's big car."

"Because you also want to take your motorcycle to the mountains."

"Why not? Grandma promised that it won't be the motorcycle that kills me, right?"

"Yes."

"So if the weather is good, I'll ride up into the mountains on the motorcycle, to find the little village where my mother gave birth to me during the War."

"You know the place?"

"I'll find it."

And he leads her to her room, covers her with a down blanket, and when he sees her toes poking from under it, he takes thick woolen socks from the drawer, and before putting them on her, he brings her feet close to his lips and kisses them lightly. It's going to be a cold night, he says, and warm feet keep the body warm even if the blanket comes off while you sleep.

"And the appendage?"

"The appendage?" He gets confused. "What about it?"

"Maybe we'll freeze it in the mountains, in the place you were born."

And he laughs at the notion that the threat nestled in his head can also be a source of amusement.

She plunges into a deep sleep after a long and exhausting day, then gradually the great cathedral emerges, devoid of paintings and stained glass and statues and ornaments, and in the vast empty space, whose walls incorporate the ancient Roman wall, stands the altar, and Sabrina in a white dress, with a golden chalice in her hand. In the dream, a searing pain persists that a Jewish girl who will move to Israel is allowed to sing in a church, and even become the Mother of God. It is a pain so searing that smoke rises in the dark from the glittering chalice, as if the wine had caught fire, and the smell of smoke grows stronger, until it wakes her and she sits up in bed in a panic. The snowstorm has tapered off, and the church tower near their home wears a white kippah. In the hush that has descended on the world only Papà's voice is heard, scorched and tormented, trying to pry from his mother in Venice just what the doctor said, the director of the hospital, her former lover. And Rachele goes back to bed and covers her head with the blanket to escape the smoke wafting through the apartment. Too bad I didn't throw away all the cigarettes in the rain, she agonizes, even as slumber again shuts off her consciousness.

6

It's the first morning of New Year's vacation, and although she is entitled to sweet, boundless slumber, Rachele is roused early. Tomorrow, in the Dolomites, she can doze to her heart's content, but this morning they must finish packing and not be late for lunch at her mother's parents,' since by afternoon Nonno needs to be at the church, to make preparations for the Midnight Mass.

"Will Papà come too?"

"Yes, Nonno bought a special present that'll help him."

"Help him with what? The illness?"

"Do not say illness, that's only a thought . . ."

"Okay, just a thought . . . But where is he now?"

"In the garage with Paolo, working on the trailer for the motorcycle."

"What's there to work on? We've towed it a zillion times."

"True, but Paolo wants more than blinking lights, he now insists putting brake lights on the trailer. Stop asking questions, there's no time, you have to get up, and why on earth did you sleep with socks on?"

"Papà told me to put them on, he believes that warm feet preserve body heat."

"Wrong. After a day of walking, feet deserve to breathe freely at night."

But Rachele waves her long legs in the air, pedaling an imaginary bicycle. Look, I'm getting them ready for the mountains. At first it seemed that three suitcases would suffice, but the forecast of cold and snow, prospect of parties, and especially New Year's Eve, fill a fourth valise. And really, why not? Paolo's car is big, the hotel rooms are spacious, and the bellboys are quick to carry bags and provide other services. Thus before noon, as the sky clears but the temperature falls, the four suitcases stand ready in the corridor. A taxi waits to pick up the daughter and granddaughter for the holiday meal at the home of the grandparents, who live in the old part of town, not far from the train station, in a housing project built after the World War for railroad workers.

The house isn't large, so order is strictly maintained. On the lower floor is the living room, with access to a garden,

and on the upper floor is a master bedroom with a small
room beside it. When her parents travel to social events
in Milan or Venice, especially if they extend their trip by
a night or two, Rachele prefers to sleep in this little house,
and not at Grandpa Sergio's grand apartment. But because
the tiny dimensions of the room make her anxious, Nonno
yields his side of the big double bed, takes down the crucifix
from the wall and hangs it in the small room, while Rachele
bounces in the huge bed beside her Nonna. She loves this
grandmother, a devout atheist who is nonetheless careful
not to sabotage the Jewish faith of her only granddaughter.
How is it you don't mind, Nonna, Rachele keeps asking,
that your Christian daughter turned into a Jew? Because in
the World War, the Jews lost so many people, they had to be
compensated with a few Italians as a gift. But that's not just
any gift, Rachele insists, these are Italians who are switch-
ing their god. There is no God, declares Nonna dismissively,
and there's nothing to switch. Nothing changes, everyone
is only human in the end. If so, Rachele persists, why do
you, a nonbeliever, still go to church on Christmas? Not
because of some god, says Nonna, I go for the singing and
music. I don't kneel, I don't open the missal, I sit as in a the-
ater to demonstrate that for me, prayer is just a show.

Rachele hugs Nonna tightly and tells her she ate a light
breakfast so that she'd be hungry at lunch. I adore your

food, when I graduate the two of us will open a restaurant. Although the Luzzatto family is not strict about the kosher laws, Nonna Paola is wary of tripping them up with a violation of some obscure dietary restriction, and so devises dishes that evade the obstacles erected by generations of rabbis. Over the years she has perfected her fish, pastas of many colors, soups hot and cold, generous salads, glorious desserts—a bounty of food taken from the oven, stovetop, or refrigerator with clockwork timing, like the trains leaving the nearby station.

Papà phones to say he'll be late, so please start the lunch without him. His absence enables the grandparents to get a clearer idea of their son-in-law's medical condition. They listen to their daughter's gloomy report, welcoming with a smile their granddaughter's diagnosis, that maybe it's a kind of appendage enlarging the brain to help Papà understand the changing situation. Slightly comforted by their granddaughter's brilliant notion, they write down in the new year's calendar the date of her bat mitzvah, and ask for details of the synagogue ceremony, whether they will be permitted to sit among the Jews at prayer.

"If you just put a little kippah on your head, Nonno," says Rachele, "nobody will bother you, you will not be invited to go up to the *bima* and say the Torah blessings, but you and Nonna can't sit together, she'll sit in the balcony with the women."

"And what will you do at this celebration? What's your role?"

"I have to recite a prayer in Hebrew, by heart, a prayer the rabbi is teaching me."

"A prayer we won't understand."

"So if you like, I can sing you the beginning in Hebrew, that I already know by heart, and I'll translate it into Italian for you." And Rachele stands by the window and begins to sing the *Aleinu* prayer:

> It is our duty to praise the Lord of all, to ascribe
> greatness to the author of creation,
> Who has not made us like the nations of the lands,
> nor placed us like the families of the earth,
> Who has not made our portion like theirs, nor our
> destiny like all their multitudes.
> For they worship vanity and emptiness, and pray to
> a god who cannot save.
> But we bow in worship and give thanks unto the
> Supreme King of kings . . .

Nonno claps his hands and says, it sounds strong and persuasive, maybe because I don't understand a word. In any case, what's the essence here? Rachele starts to translate, stammers and stops.

But the first few words are enough for her Nonno

to guess the spirit of the prayer and its intention, he's not angry, just amused. So, it's basically a prayer against us, against the Christians, a fitting prayer for your celebration, luckily it will be chanted in Hebrew and not Italian, otherwise there'll be guests who might feel insulted. But no, no, Grandpa, no, says Rachele, turning red, it's not against you or Catholics, just against idol worshippers. And you're not idol worshippers.

"Actually we are," laughs Nonna, her eyes flashing, "the Catholics are idol worshippers, think how many statues they have in their churches. But no problem, dear, I like your prayer, it's a brave prayer, don't be afraid to recite it."

Papà arrives, tired, his eyes sunken. It turned out that affixing brake lights to the rear of the motorcycle trailer was impossible, but since Paolo insisted that the tow not hide the brake lights, they dismantled one of the car's rear lights and installed it in the upper part of the rear window, so that a driver behind them could follow their every zig and zag. But someone must sit beside that brake light, to make sure it doesn't slip away during the trip.

Nonna quickly brings an elaborate lunch for Papà, but he ignores most of it, focusing ravenously on the spaghetti. Why didn't you teach your daughter to cook like you? I taught her, but since you people mostly eat in restaurants, she quickly forgot what she had learned.

The day is short and the drive is long, and Nonno promised to help with holiday decorations in the church, so now is the time for presents. Papà tears open the gift wrapping and discovers a colorful plastic map of the Italian and Tyrolean Alps along the Austrian border. A rigid, waterproof map that folds easily but doesn't wrinkle. A map of highways and dirt roads, hiking trails and ski slopes, identifying tiny villages and isolated inns. Papà is moved by the gift and hugs his father-in-law. Wonderful, Ernesto, fabulous, you couldn't have chosen a more useful gift.

Mamma's parents enrich her collection of statuettes with a bronze of a Roman lad, lean and muscular, which if not truly ancient can still fit in with the statuettes that stand in a row in the dining room vitrine. Two presents await Rachele, not just one. The first arrived this morning straight from the farmers' market: a gilded cage containing a merry, colorful little parrot, which will stay at Nonno and Nonna's till Rachele returns from vacation. They'll need to find someone to explain how to care for it, and determine whether it could speak in two languages. The second present is from Nonna, who found a copy of *Cuore* by Edmondo De Amicis, an old edition from before the World War, a large, lavish volume, filled with illustrations, whose thick pages can, if necessary, soak up the tears.

Rachele is excited and confused. She hugs and kisses her grandfather, then pounces emotionally on her Nonna and covers her face with kisses. You're a real Grandma, Rachele says, voice trembling. You are honest and brave.

7

As twilight ushers in the end of the day, Paolo's car waits outside their home, and the motorcycle sits on the trailer, protected by a tarpaulin tailored to its dimensions. The car is an old English Land Rover, wide and heavy, in which young Brits tooled around France and Italy in the 1980s, but when they landed in Venice they got into a row so terrible that the friendship was over and they had to sell their car. At the time, Paolo, who owned a luxurious gondola in Venice, was thinking of moving his business from the water to dry land, and sought a vehicle both strong and inexpensive. The Land Rover attracted few buyers and he seized the moment, rented out his gondola, and bought the English field car for a ridiculously low price. He painted it black in memory of the gondola, and began gradually to change its identity. After taking care of auto registration and insurance, he moved the steering from the right side to the left. But he neglected the speedometer and gauges for oil pressure and the cooling system, which remained on the right side, and sometimes, so a passenger can feel like a co-pilot, Paolo will ask them to report the numbers on the dashboard, to test their accuracy and confirm that the car doesn't speed.

The strength and width of the English car allowed its Italian owner to serve passengers in the Italian and Austrian Alps, as well as make city trips for selected customers. Despite its size and rigidity, the grandmother, Riccardo's mother, preferred it to a regular taxi, since an old lady doesn't need a soft, fast car, but rather an oversized vehicle she can get into easily, and also because Paolo was alert to her wishes and always adapted accordingly.

The four suitcases descend one by one, the motorcycle helmet bouncing among them. And because the taillight, uprooted from its customary place and assigned to the rear window, needs supervision, the father and mother are dispatched to the back seat to ensure that it doesn't slide from its new location. Rachele settles into the front seat and the driver fastens her safety belt, careful to keep it snug but not uncomfortable.

Paolo has known Rachele since her childhood, thanks to the winter drives to the Dolomites, and in summer to the beach in Naples, and also because now and then the grandmother sends him to bring her granddaughter to Venice for no special reason, not merely when her parents are on a long vacation. For the Venetian Grandma, Rachele is her only true grandchild; the grandchildren of men who enjoyed her favors are not as worthy of her affection.

Few are the trucks on Christmas Eve, buses too are rare, and the roads feel festive. Many homes and shops display Christmas trees bedecked with glittering decorations, and in the churches humble crucifixes are bathed in glorious light. Paolo is curious about the gifts his young passenger received from her Catholic grandparents. Not both of them, Rachele corrects him, because only Nonno still believes in Jesus, Nonna has given up on him. Paolo smiles. Even if she doesn't believe in him, your Grandma gives you a present on his birthday. True, confirms Rachele, not one present but two, a parrot with a green tail, who knows a few words of Italian, and Rachele will try to teach it Hebrew as a second language, and an old book of stories that's still important. Important in what sense? Because it's *Cuore*, which was written to educate the youth but adults can also learn some humanity from it. *Cuore*? Paolo ponders the name. It can't be that Paolo doesn't know the famous book, which is read in every Italian school. Apparently you just forgot the name. But Paolo is not to blame for his ignorance, he had a beautiful singing voice, and in childhood his father would let him skip classes to entertain passengers in the gondola. So he barely went to school. As a boy you sang in the gondola? The girl's eyes sparkle. You never told me. Because you never asked me about my childhood. Not only did I not read *Heart*, I missed a lot of other books too. I was busy with other things. Look how your father is already asleep, and soon your mother will join him. The tests yesterday in Venice depressed them so much they're afraid to catch a glimpse of the city. But you, sweet girl, don't pass it up, turn your head and see how gorgeous this city is on Christmas Eve.

Venice is revealed in full splendor. The domes of the basilicas and turrets of the towers are all aglow, between the masts of ships at anchor, Italian and foreign, are strings of colored lights, and in the distance, fireworks fly above the Lido. Where will you sleep tonight, Paolo? With us in the hotel, or a different hotel? Your father wanted me to be at the same hotel as you, but I didn't want him to spend the money, since I'll be driving back early in the morning. So we found a simple place, close to the church. Church?

Why? You'll also pray at Midnight Mass? Yes, but only if I find a good meal before the prayers, because on an empty stomach it is hard to believe a divine baby was born in a stable, of all places.

The road begins to climb into the Dolomites, and with the first hills that appear on their right, Venice disappears. If you want to nap like your parents, I can lean your seat back and cover you with a blanket. But Rachele wants to hear about Paolo's childhood, and whether his father really took him from class so he could entertain tourists with songs. Yes, and I knew other folk songs, and was in demand in other gondolas too. But how is it that we, who've known you so many years, never knew that you were let out of school so you could sing? Because you didn't take an interest in me and never asked about my childhood, and almost nothing about my life today. They tell me you're a diligent student, but you shouldn't look down on kids who barely went to school. Even without formal learning I'm not just a driver, I'm also a licensed tour guide, and I know roads and trails in Italy that even your father, who loves to explore, hasn't heard of. Here, for example, you've traveled on this road to the Dolomites lots of times, in winter and summer, by day and by night, but I bet you haven't a clue, and not just because it's nighttime, where we are, or what village we're soon going to pass. Who says I don't know? Rachele protests. You'd be surprised. The village is Conegliano.

"Wrong. Conegliano is another half hour away, but now, in ten minutes' time, what village will we pass? Do you know?"

"Maybe Pordenone."

"Pordenone?" Paolo laughs. "No, it's not on this road, to get there you have to turn right after Conegliano. You see, you've been on this road a thousand times, they say you're a good student, and you still don't know the name of the city we're getting close to."

"Maybe Treviso? Yes, Treviso."

"Now finally you got something right. The little lights in the distance, that's Treviso."

And the driver, challenging the famous book he never heard of, continues to bombard Rachele with the names of the places they pass or will soon pass in the darkness. And because Rachele has failed the roads test she tries to suggest that she doesn't need to know the names of towns and villages in Italy, because it's possible that she, like her friend Sabrina, will in the future live in a country that's more suitable for Jews. But Paolo won't let up. Italy is your homeland, whether you like it or not, Italian is your mother tongue, and you were born in a country the whole world is attracted to, so you have to keep Italy inside you even if you leave it. Keeping it not just in the titles of old books, but in the names of villages, mountains, and lakes.

It's getting colder, snow flurries flashing in the headlights like a rain of stars. They illuminate the driver's handsome face as he is overcome by his love of the homeland. Rachele checks the numbers shining in the three English dials and asks the driver, would he not like to know what the dials say? He laughs, oh dear girl, I can feel what they say very well, even without looking, but if you want to give me a report I can confirm that what I feel is right.

And in her soft, but clear voice, the Jewish girl provides the data. And Paolo says, I also feel that it's getting colder, and he pulls to the roadside, and takes two thick wool blankets from the boot. He first bundles up the bright-eyed girl, then spreads the second blanket on her parents, sleeping side by side.

Only when the swirling snow makes the tires squeal do they pull apart, and Riccardo, who can identify every spot on the way to Cortina d'Ampezzo, says, unbelievable, Paolo, you are a wonderful driver to have managed to take us straight to the hotel so safely and gently. I helped, announces Rachele, because I didn't fall asleep like you did, and I talked with Paolo the whole way and made sure he wouldn't also fall asleep.

It's almost midnight, and the hotel waits for the arrival of the Jewish guests. Because the dinner hour has passed, covered trays of food have been left in the two rooms. Paolo takes Rachele's suitcase to her room, lifts the cover of the tray and says, nice, you won't go to bed hungry. But what about you? How will you manage to find a meal so you won't be hungry at Midnight Mass? Please, Paolo, take my meal, Nonna Paola filled me up at lunch with fabulous Italian food, and I want to keep tasting it even in my sleep.

8

A sudden snowstorm blows in overnight, and in the morning hotel guests are warned against skiing in low visibility. But by ten o'clock the skies are clearing and Papà says: There are only seven days till New Year's, and who knows what the sky has in store for us. So even if it clears only briefly, that mustn't be missed. And it's possible that after the appendage has been removed from my brain the art of skiing will have vanished along with it.

Riccardo has grown fond of the name his daughter gave his brain tumor, and he enjoys repeating it not just to his wife and daughter but also to Jewish and Italian friends, some of whom heed the Jew's call to take advantage of the clear sky to ride up in the cable car and ski back down to the hotel. Mamma no longer skis, but Rachele, who has skied since age seven, will stick by her father. If skiing by Jews on Christmas is a tribute to the birth of a divine child in the Holy Land, why shouldn't she join in? And she surprises them all with a pair of red skis on her shoulder, a red wool scarf, red boots and a red windbreaker; even her sunglasses have a red frame. What's this, Papà wonders, you decided to dress like Little Red Riding Hood? I didn't choose all this red stuff, your mother did, so you can't lose me in the mountains.

"I could lose you?" he protests. "Why does my mother always insist on scaring people?"

The cable car fills with skiers. Empty cars bump downhill, having deposited bold early risers, undaunted by the storm. Several skiers who know Riccardo Luzzatto take an interest in his red daughter. Who gave her those curls? She found them herself, Papà laughs, even now, it's unclear where. When she was born her mother said it was a mistake, this isn't my baby, in our entire family there are no curls like these, but I disagreed. There are indeed no curls like these in the Luzzatto family, but her mouth is a copy of mine, the mouth of a lawyer who convinces judges.

Rachele shakes her head resentfully. She doesn't want to be a lawyer, she wants to be a judge who sits silently while everyone fears her verdict. But who needs a courtroom anyway? Maybe she'll work in a zoo. She pulls her wool cap down to cover her curls, looks up to see if the sky is still blue and finds that the strong winter sun has added a golden sheen.

At the top, everyone is quick to put on their skis, trying to squeeze in an additional run. Papà checks the bindings of his daughter's skis and says: I'll take the black run and you the blue as always, and we'll meet at the bottom at the cafeteria, and if the sky stays clear we'll take another run. Rachele grabs his hand. But you're not well, so don't ski the steepest run, do the red instead? No, he protests, there's no connection here with the illness. He heads off to the right, following other skiers, plants his poles in the snow and disappears.

She takes the blue route, moderate and gentle, its twists and curves at friendly angles, alongside older skiers, or boys and girls with their instructors. Ahead of her, not wearing a helmet, is a curly-headed golden-haired boy. For a moment Rachele thinks it's Enrico, the one sent by the principal to get her, and she speeds up to see, but it's a different boy, who picks up speed to outrun the foreign girl.

Papà drinks cappuccino at the café near the cable car terminal. It was fantastic, he says, your appendage only sharpens the pleasure. My appendage? Why mine? Never mind, smiles Papà. You invented the word, sweetie, don't be a sourpuss who can't take a joke. It's not a joke, she mutters, it can't be a joke. True, says Papà, it's no joke. Come, I'll get you something to eat. No, says Rachele, just a drink, order me a double espresso. Very good, it will be your fuel for another run, we can't let this glorious sky go to waste.

Rachele gulps down her espresso and she and her father get into the cable car. The afternoon sun is perched at the summit. The glow in the sky, say the skiers, feels more Easter than Christmas. Riccardo is excited too. Jesus accepts with joy and gratitude the Jews skiing in his honor, he whispers to a friend, who recoils and turns away. Riccardo casts his eyes upward, follows the cable to the very top, fluffy clouds floating above. This spot is accessible only by chair lift, shuttling slowly on a circular cable.

"Listen, Rachele, the sky is so generous today that I feel a need to ski from the top. I've done it many times, who knows if I'll get another chance. You ski your blue run, and we'll meet at the bottom, and you may find me waiting for you again, because the run from the top is fast as hell."

"Don't go up there," she warns, "you're ill, and the run is really steep. When you get well you'll ski to the sky and back, not today. Mamma will be angry with me if I let you."

"Mamma doesn't mind. She trusts me."

"Maybe my Mamma, but not yours, not Grandma . . . She'll be furious with me if she finds out I didn't stop you."

"If you don't tell her, she won't be furious. But why are you scared? It's a safe run, and in another half hour the sky won't be clear."

"So I'll wait for you here."

"Why?"

"So you don't get overexerted on the steep run. Stop here, and we'll continue as before, you on the black and me on blue."

"You're just being stubborn. All right, we'll see if I can even stop here. Don't wait too long for me."

As he talks, he grabs hold of the slow-moving chair lift, sits down, and soon vanishes in the heights of the white mountain.

Rachele waits, removing her helmet, taking her skis off, hugging herself for warmth. A cable car arrives and discharges its jolly skiers, and Rachele again spots the golden-haired boy who resembles Enrico. He is again without a helmet, and when she sees him waiting his turn in the queue for the blue route, she feels the urge to ski beside him. Why wait for Papà, who might easily forget his promise in the rush of skiing? But what if he stops here? What'll he think? That she doesn't care about him anymore.

It gets colder. The skies grow darker, scattered hailstones lashing. Fewer people now. She hunches over, pulls the red ski cap down to her face. What happened yesterday at the class play in the church? Did anyone come see it, apart from the teachers? A cable car arrives from below, half empty. Because it's lunchtime soon, or because of the weather? She closes her eyes. Instead of curling up indoors in a warm blanket, she stands alone, waiting for a father who has apparently forgotten her.

Five minutes, ten, fifteen. Fewer and fewer people. The hail is stronger now. A cable car ascends empty and descends empty. Sparked by anxiety, she dons the helmet, shoulders her skis, and watches the empty chairs going up and down, then grabs hold of an approaching chair and jumps onto it. Her legs sway in the air as she takes off into the fog.

She's alone in the carousel of chairs, no one aboard, up or down. And when she gets to the top, she misses the moment to jump off the moving chair, and if not for the beer-bellied lift attendant who pulls her off, she'd be on her way back down. What's happening, girl? What are you doing here? This run is closed. I didn't come to ski, I came to look for my father, Signor Luzzatto, who came up here. Do you remember him? Why should anybody here remember your father? If we take the trouble to remember everyone who gets off the lift and disappears downhill, says the attendant, we won't have room in our memory even for a lady in red like you.

But Rachele insists on at least seeing the place where the ski run begins. And the attendant guides her up a ladder to a small wooden platform with a view of a route marked by red flags, winding through the valley amid bushes and trees, vanishing and reappearing, until it reaches a big white building in the distance, smoke rising from its three chimneys, presumably the hotel. Listen, Signore, she says to the attendant, who enjoys her company, it doesn't look especially scary, and it apparently goes straight to our hotel, and since I've come way up here, I may as well ski down, I've been skiing since I was seven. And she takes the skis down from her shoulder, but the attendant quickly pulls them away.

"You're not skiing anywhere from here, not to Papà and Mamma or Nonno and Nonna."

He sticks two fingers in his mouth and produces a mischievous whistle, and a young man in khaki overalls emerges from the station's hut. Look who I found. Red

Riding Hood is looking for her father, now she wants to ski to him. Ski? Now? In this wind? She's nuts. Come on, we'll take her to her father. And the lift attendant helps her climb down from the little wooden platform, leads her to a snow caterpillar, and puts her in the back seat. The young bearded guy, after closing the station, sits down at the wheel, but before starting the engine he asks: What's your name, in case somebody wants to know. Rachele, she says proudly. Rachele what? Rachele Luzzatto. Luzzatto? the young man inquires, what kind of name is that? It's a name of Jews from Venice, says the older man. Really? The young man is impressed. You're a Jew? Rachele nods. If so, the young man says to his friend, we better take good care of her, so they won't blame us, too, for abandoning Jews.

The snowcat tractor grinds noisily down the slope, and the bearded driver sings into the wind. The girl takes off her helmet and holds onto her red ski cap with both hands so it won't fly off. You should know, Signorina, says the older lift attendant, that the driver here is also a singer, he sings in a choir. Too bad you didn't hear him at Midnight Mass.

They drop her off in front of the hotel and wait till she rests her skis in the rack and goes inside. She crosses the lobby, teeming with guests waiting for the dining room to open. She hunts for her mother, spots her sitting in a corner chatting with her non-Jewish friends. Where's Papà?

she asks. In the bar, says the mother. She finds her father, drinking with friends, and lets him have it: Hello, Judas Iscariot. Without waiting for an answer, she strides into the kitchen and requests that room service deliver her lunch.

In her room she peels off her ski gear and clothing, showers in hot water, and greets the bellman in a bathrobe. The meal is delicious and she leaves not a crumb on the tray. When she's already under the blankets, Papà pounds on the door, irately: What's with Judas Iscariot?

"Because I waited for you and you didn't come, and you didn't care where I was."

"But I told you not to wait. How could I get to you if the trail from the top doesn't pass by there? I trusted you to manage on your own."

"You're right. I went to the top and saw that you couldn't get to where I was waiting."

"You went to the top alone?"

"Because I wanted to understand why you didn't come as you promised."

"Are you crazy? How'd you get down from there?"

"The lift attendants brought me back in their tractor."

"In which case, why did you call me Judas in front of everyone?"

"No reason," smiles Rachele. "What's the problem? Wasn't he a Jew?"

Papà looks at the empty food tray. Tell me, you don't

feel any pity for me? She says nothing, her face turning red, tears suddenly flooding her eyes.

"No, I don't feel pity, but I am very, very worried."

Papà strokes her head and leaves.

She locks the door, turns on the bedside lamp, pulls the blanket higher, picks up the copy of *Heart* that Nonna gave her, and finds the page they were at when she was plucked from class, in the story about the boy who mistook a stranger for his unconscious father, and cared for him day after day.

> It was four o'clock in the afternoon, and just as the boy had abandoned himself to one of these outbursts of tenderness and hope, a sound of footsteps became audible outside the nearest door in the ward, and a strong voice pronounced two words only—"Farewell, Sister!"—which made him spring to his feet, a cry repressed in his throat.
>
> At that moment there entered the ward a man with a thick bandage on his hand, followed by a nurse.
>
> The boy uttered a sharp cry, and stood rooted to the spot.
>
> The man turned round, looked at him for

a moment, and uttered a cry in his turn—
"Cicillo!"—and darted towards him.

The boy fell into his father's arms, choking with
emotion.

The nuns, the nurses, and the doctor's assistant
ran up, and stood there in amazement.

The boy could not recover his voice.

"Oh, my Cicillo!" exclaimed the father, after
bestowing an attentive look at the sick man, as he
kissed the boy repeatedly. "Cicillo, my son, how
is this? They took you to the bedside of another
man. And there was I, in despair over not seeing
you after Mamma had written me: 'I've sent him.'
Poor Cicillo! How many days have you been here?
How did this mistake occur? I recovered easily! I
have a good constitution, you know! And how is
Mamma? And Concettella? And the little baby—
how are they all? I am leaving the hospital now.
Come, then. Oh, Lord God! Who would have
thought it!"

The boy tried to interpolate a few words of
family news. "Oh how happy I am!" he stammered.
"How happy I am! What terrible days I have
passed!" And he could not stop kissing his father.

But he stayed put.

"Come," said his father, "we can get home by this

evening." And he drew the lad towards him. The boy turned to look at his patient.

"Well, are you coming or not?" his father demanded, in amazement.

The boy cast yet another glance at the sick man, who opened his eyes at that moment and gazed intently at him.

Then a flood of words poured from his very soul. "No, father; wait—here—I can't. Here is this old man. I have been here for five days. He gazes at me incessantly. I thought he was you. I love him dearly. He looks at me; I give him his drink; he wants me always beside him; he is very ill now. Have patience; I have not the courage—I don't know—it pains me too much; I will return home tomorrow; let me stay here a little longer; I don't want to leave him. See how he looks at me! I don't know who he is, but he needs me; he will die alone: let me stay here, dear father!"

"Bravo, little fellow!" exclaimed the doctor's assistant.

The father stood in perplexity, staring at the boy; then he looked at the sick man. "Who is he?" he inquired.

"A farmer, like yourself," replied the doctor's assistant, "not from here, but who entered the hospital on the very day you entered it. He was out of his senses when they brought him here, and could not speak. Perhaps he has a family far away, and sons. He probably thinks that your son is one of his."

The sick man was still looking at the boy.

The father said to Cicillo, "Stay."

"He will not have to stay much longer," murmured the doctor's assistant.

"Stay," repeated his father: "you have heart. I will go home immediately, to relieve Mamma's distress. Here's a little money for your expenses. Goodbye, my brave little son, until we meet again!"

9

Two nights later she dreams of sitting in a hospital, taking care of someone. She plunges into sleep so deep that dreams dissolve into nothingness. Only one dream floats to the surface, perhaps because it takes place in a big church turned into a hospital, a church whose believers suffer ski injuries, with plaster casts on their arms and legs, walking with crutches, or lying in bed and chattering merrily. Among them, amazingly, are two ultra-Orthodox Jews, dressed in black, who have managed to slide their sidelocks from under the bandages wrapped around their fractured skulls. So Papà is right, it's no joke, skiing on Christmas is a Jewish prayer of thanks for the birth of a baby who will save the goyim.

And perhaps because of the long dream Rachele arrives at breakfast just as her parents are about to finish. What happened, her mother taunts her, again dreams that you didn't want to end? I wanted to, they didn't want to but I've already forgotten them. She did remember the dream about the church that turned into a hospital but preferred not to mention it so that Papà wouldn't say, see, even in dreams you're attracted to churches.

Bright morning light pours into the big dining room windows. The skies are benevolent today, says the mother, if you hurry you can ski three or four runs. Papà gazes silently at the map of roads and trails that Nonno Ernesto gave him, and with the aid of a butter knife and the scale listed on the map, he calculates distances.

"Today you ski alone," her mother says, "because Papà decided to make a motorcycle ride to the village where he was born during the War. He finally persuaded Grandma to give him the name."

"Why didn't she tell him till now?"

"Because during the War Grandpa Sergio left her alone in such a godforsaken place that she was embarrassed to speak its name."

"I can't believe it. What's so embarrassing about it?"

"Ask her. With you she speaks frankly."

"How come she agreed all of a sudden to give him the name?"

"Because Papà said that before he dies he wants to see if he was actually born."

"What?"

Riccardo looks up from the map and smiles.

"You don't get his humor," says the mother, steering her daughter to the breakfast buffet. "Take the eggs, the cheese, croissants, and vegetables, but not the sausages. You promised your rabbi that at least until your bat mitzvah you'll keep . . ."

"The sausages are pork?"

"What else? You thought they were lamb or goat?"

"But you ate them."

"We're post–bar mitzvah," growls Papà, his eyes still glued to the map.

When Rachele returns to the table she notices the leather jacket draped on her father's chair, and under it the black motorcycle helmet, and as she nibbles her croissant she decides she wants to go with her father, to sit behind him on the motorcycle, hugging him. Really, why not? Many times, en route to school or the rabbi's lesson, she has leaned into his back on the bike and held onto his hips.

"How many kilometers from here to where you were born, if you were actually born?"

"That's what I'm trying to figure out. It's hard to estimate, because the road twists and turns in the mountains, but my guess is the village is no more than eight or nine kilometers away."

"So why not ask Paolo to drive you there?" Mamma says.

"Because a large car could easily get stuck on those narrow roads. Why else would I tow the motorcycle the whole way here?"

"If so," Rachele interrupts, "take me with you."

"Don't be silly," Mamma objects.

"I also want to see the place where Papà entered the world."

"What's to see? Obviously a poor, tiny village, if your grandmother is ashamed of it."

Rachele looks closely at her father to gauge his reaction, but he's still poring over the map.

"Why ride by motorcycle on bumpy, unreliable roads, when the weather is perfect for the skiing you love so much?"

"The skiing won't go away, but this is a one-time chance to see where Papà was born."

"Is that so important? You've been waiting for months for Christmas vacation. Tomorrow the fog and rain will be back."

"Tomorrow? How do you know what the weather will be like tomorrow? Maybe tomorrow will be nice too, Mamma, but I'll never have another chance to see this place, which is maybe five kilometers from here."

"Nine," says Papà, glancing fondly at his daughter, radiant after her good night's sleep.

"So nine. Papà is a careful rider, I've ridden with him a thousand times, and you didn't mind, Mamma, so why do you mind now?"

"Because it's in the mountains, on dangerous roads. Anyway, how can you ride on a motorcycle without a helmet?"

"With my ski helmet."

"But that's a helmet for snow. You have to have a real helmet."

"Where would we get a real helmet this morning?"

"Nowhere, which is why you're staying here."

"But . . ."

"Even so," Riccardo interrupts, "why shouldn't she come with me?"

"Only with a proper helmet, I haven't the strength to deal with another broken head in the family."

"Broken?" Riccardo is taken aback. "But where can we get her a helmet?"

"You agreed, against my wishes, that a girl of twelve should take a perilous motorcycle ride in the mountains, so you have to find her a real helmet. You always know how to find what you want."

And indeed, Papà borrows a helmet from one of the waiters, but because it was meant for a head bigger than his daughter's, he himself will wear it, and he will fit his helmet to her head. She is sent off to switch her ski jacket for a woolen sweater-vest and her mother's raincoat. The gleaming motorcycle awaits them in front of the hotel, and after gunning the engine to a roar, the father invites his daughter to get on board.

The motorcycle carries them past Monte Marmolada, navigating the narrow, twisting roads. Now and again Riccardo stops at a fork, unfolds the map his Catholic father-in-law gave him, and confirms the way to his birthplace. Rivers and waterfalls abound, cables hum overhead, skiers wave hello from cable cars, and a solitary snowboarder glides above them on his way to the valley. Frosty vapors cling to fresh wildflowers, hunks of snow fall from the trees. They pass roadhouses where hikers and skiers sit at tables and sip wine from ceramic mugs. And invariably one of the patrons rises from his seat to check out the glamorous motorcycle and the riders, a man and a girl. Riccardo just waves and rides on, looking for signs pointing in the right direction. The nine kilometers measured on the dining room table have turned into fifteen, but not more. The map wasn't wrong, but maybe the measurer's hand was unsteady. The name of the village is displayed in Italian and German on a red wooden sign in the snow. This is it, shouts the father to the daughter who warms her face on his back. This is the place I came into the world, and not from the Holy Spirit.

Village children run after the motorcycle, pointing the way to the school, where the teacher Alfredo is waiting, as agreed. He will take them to his elderly father, an Austrian physician, who in the last year of the War, in midwinter, got an emergency call from a hotel in the Dolomites—an Italian woman but also Jewish, her life threatened by the fetus in her womb. As a result, the mother whose life he saved makes an annual gift to the local school, via the doctor's son Alfredo, for repairs and renovations. The doctor, her savior, would not accept the money for himself.

The father and his daughter take off their helmets and enter the living room of a small wooden house to meet the doctor, who lately turned ninety. The room is dark, lit only by two dim bulbs in the corners. The old man suffers from eye disease that gets progressively worse in the light, so he mostly sits in the dark, listening to classical music. His son the teacher brings him news of the illuminated world.

Riccardo bows to the old man and sits next to him, carefully trying to extract the details of his birth fifty-six years past. But the Tyrolean Italian dialect spoken by the teacher, of which Rachele catches only a few words, turns into pure Austrian German when the doctor speaks.

"Why won't he speak Italian?" Riccardo asks.

"Out of Austrian patriotism. He says that our village was always Austrian and not Italian, and only after the Great War the Italians annexed it without justification, since after all, the Italians were Nazis too, like the Germans and Japanese."

"Nazis? The Italians?" Riccardo is amused by the old man's extreme analogy. "Maybe you mean Fascists."

"That's not the same?"

"Not really," says Riccardo, "only similar."

The doctor points to Rachele and mumbles something.

"My father asks who this girl is."

"She's my daughter, granddaughter of the woman whose life you saved."

The old man nods with recognition. She does remind

him a little of that woman, except that woman was more beautiful.

"When she grows up," the father promises, "she'll be even more beautiful than her grandmother."

The son translates the prediction of beauty into German, but the Austrian who sits in the dark has his doubts about the future.

Now comes the question that motivated the Jew to come all the way out here. How is it that an Austrian patriot was willing, in those days of war, to save a Jewish woman from death and deliver her baby. Even before the son finishes translating the question, the old man has a ready answer, and the speed of his reply suggests he has long expected that one fine day the baby himself would show up to pose the question, if not necessarily on a motorcycle.

So, Signor Luzzatto—the teacher translates his father's Austrian reply into Tyrolean Italian—a young Jewish woman, in the ninth month of pregnancy, was brought to him from the Italian Dolomites on Christmas of 1943, when our village was in low spirits. People knew what befell the Wehrmacht at Stalingrad, and they lost confidence that the Germans would ultimately put the world in proper order, and every nation exactly where it belonged. When the young Jewish woman in danger of death came here, the doctor, on the other hand, was still sure the German army would overcome the disaster in Russia and conquer Moscow, and the Jewish woman and her baby might yet be sent to the final place for all the Jews. But he also thought—the son continues to translate—that if, and only if, the disaster inflicted by the Bolsheviks aroused the rebelliousness of other nations, a Jewish woman with a baby a German ushered into the world could redound to the credit of his family and the village in the minds of those who after the War will think that Germany should be punished for the mistakes of Hitler's generals.

Rachele whispers in her father's ear: What's he talking about? Later, whispers back Riccardo, shocked, excited, amused, upset by the doctor's candid explanation. Whereas the teacher, confused and embarrassed, translating for his father, decides to hurry up and end the meeting. He turns out one of the corner lights, deepening the darkness of the room. My poor father has holes in his retinas, he says, and strong light harms his brain pan. He suggests the father and daughter, their helmets under their arms, come up to the third floor, where the birth took place. Riccardo would have liked to chat with the doctor some more, perhaps provoke further morsels of malice, but the teacher insists that it's time to say goodbye, so there's no choice but to shake hands with the old Nazi who brought him into the world and go up with his daughter and the teacher to the third floor, to a room bare of furniture and all else except a rocking horse. Outside the wide-open window, facing north, is a view of the Austrian Alps, a primeval landscape, wild, lavish, and defiant, as an inaudible wind batters a mountaintop and the afternoon sun shines like a pale diamond.

"I was really born here?" gasps Riccardo in disbelief that this breathtaking landscape was the backdrop to his birth.

"Yes, you were born here."

"But how do you know, Signore," wonders Riccardo, "were you even born yet?"

"Why not? I'm sixty."

"In other words, you were four then?"

"Exactly," confirms the village schoolteacher, who teaches not only history but arithmetic.

"You were so little, yet you remember that I was born here?"

"Yes, I was a toddler, and at first I must have thought you were the family baby and not an outsider. But my mother took you and your mother down to the cellar so your crying and shrieking would not be heard from outside—even though it's hard to tell the difference between the crying of a Jewish baby and the crying of any other baby—and I knew even then, as a four-year-old, that you didn't belong with us and should be sent back to where you did belong."

IO

The return to the hotel takes a long while, because the motorcyclist is careful not to skid on the downhill curves. And though Rachele clings to her father for dear life, he needs to be sure she hasn't fallen off. After every sharp turn he shouts, Rachelina, you still with me? She flips up the face shield of the helmet and shouts, I'm with you, drive slowly. She understood nothing of the conversation with the old doctor, but can tell that her father is in a good mood.

Lunchtime at the hotel is over. After removing his helmet and apologizing to the waiters for his dirty gear, Riccardo, undaunted, orders a meal for himself and his daughter.

The mother, hearing of their return, has come to tell them that toward evening Paolo will drive Rachele to Venice, so her Grandma can buy her a dress and shoes for the New Year's dinner party at her home tomorrow night. Venice, today? Rachele objects, Why? If Paolo takes me tomorrow morning I'll still have plenty of time to get the dress that Grandma has already picked out. There won't be enough time tomorrow, because holiday traffic will be heavy and slow, and after you buy shoes and a dress, you have to give Grandma's seamstress time enough to make alterations.

"But I don't need a new dress, and definitely not the shoes with heels Grandma wants for me. As it is, I'm one of the tallest in the class, and most of the boys are shorter than me."

"Please, Rachele, don't argue with me, she's not my Grandma, she's your Grandma. I'm not the one who decides."

"So on account of a dress I don't need, and shoes with heels I don't want, I have to give up a ski run?"

"Why forgo it? Now, look outside and you'll see there's enough light for another run. So skip dessert, get up on the mountain, because who knows if after Papà's operation we can come back here."

"What? An operation?"

"Nothing to it," Papà grins, "you won't feel a thing. Go

on, girl, don't miss the chance. Mamma will pack your suitcase."

The thought of the cold snowy mountain doesn't thrill her, but the thought of meeting the blond boy who looks like Enrico leads her to comply.

Most afternoon skiers aren't children or old folks, but young people who favor the steepest slope. She skis the gentle curves of the blue route nearly alone, stopping from time to time to check out the few faces passing by.

The Land Rover is waiting in front of the hotel, her suitcase already loaded in the back. Give me your skis, Paolo rushes her, and I'll bring them back tomorrow, and get in the car as you are, there's a ton of traffic. You can change clothes at Grandma's. But Rachele doesn't want to travel like this, and hurries to her room to change her clothes. Her parents didn't even come down to say goodbye. She heads for their room and knocks on the door angrily. Eventually her mother speaks from behind the locked door. Papà is sleeping, no point in waking him. And don't worry, I packed everything you'll need, I didn't forget a thing. What about the book, my *Heart*? I didn't forget your *Heart*, I put it in the suitcase. Besides, tomorrow morning we'll double-check that we didn't forget anything in your room. Keep calm and go along politely with

Grandma's ideas and whims. She's not always easy, but don't forget that from her point of view you are her only true grandchild.

In the car Rachele doesn't sit in front, but curls up on the back seat. This time you have to keep an eye on the dials yourself, she tells Paolo, because I'm really tired. Given no choice, the driver complies, and puts a pillow under her head, covers her with a blanket, and crisscrosses her with two safety belts.

The world darkens to greet the New Year, and two stars promptly appear. Rachele burrows into her pillow but can't fall asleep. And she decides to prove to Paolo, even as she is bound by two seat belts, unable to see the road, that she can recite from memory the names of towns and villages on the way, provided they've remained faithful to their location.

But Paolo is unimpressed. The fact that the Jews sometimes excel more than us Catholics doesn't endear them to people.

"So what should they do to be loved a little?"

"They could try taking a real interest in people who aren't rich and successful like them ... Ask about their lives, their hardships, their troubles."

"But exactly so, Paolo," exclaims Rachele, "That's exactly what I try to do with the girls in my class, but it hardly ever works."

"Maybe because you're too smart."

"Too smart? That's my fault?"

"It's not your fault, no," declares the driver, "but someone with that kind of advantage has to be especially careful and polite, to say thank you whether it's necessary or not."

"In which case, thank you, Paolo. Whether you need it or not, I'm telling you, thanks again, and thanks again and again . . ."

Meanwhile the traffic to Venice is jammed, and as the car slows down the young passenger grows drowsy, and time and distance melt away. But the joyful carousing of tourists, who have flocked to Venice from the world over to ring in the New Year, joins the bustle of ferries, tipping dreams into reality. Rachele, fearful of the year to come, hugs the pillow tightly, refusing to get up even when the wheels of the car come to a halt at the Grand Canal pier.

An Ethiopian servant awaits their arrival. He removes the suitcase from the trunk and opens the car door, and with a dazzling smile invites the granddaughter to come with him. But Paolo, unstrapping the young passenger, resists handing her over to this fellow, who has hoisted the suit-case onto his shoulder. Rather than drag the half-sleeping girl on foot through dark and narrow alleys, across canals and bridges, he whistles to a black gondola, a colorful flame burning in its bow, and carries the drowsing damsel aboard, motioning the servant to follow with the luggage. And after recommending to the young gondolier the best route to the address, he asks if he could sing a *barcarole* while he rows. But the boatman is a deaf and mute, a lip-reader, and he switches on a tape player instead. Rachele, barely awake, is aroused by a Venetian composer from three centuries past. Autumn? She guesses, but the boat-man points to the sky. Then it's Winter, says Rachele and the gondolier smiles, and to the sound of violins mim-ing the swirling wind and trickling rain, the gondola glides through narrow canals, under bridges, straight to Grandma Lara Luzzatto, who waits at her doorway.

II

What's the secret of this big house in the heart of Venice, impervious to the tumult of tourists and numerous other distractions? Do the black velvet curtains on doors and windows muffle the sound of horns of boats and *vaporetti*? Do cupboards filled with precious possessions counteract the raucous drunks outside? Even in the garden, amid shady bushes and dense foliage, one can inhale the silence.

The name of the architect is engraved on a plaque by the front door. But since he might date back to Vivaldi and Albinoni, can anyone fathom his intentions and trace his techniques? Grandma Luzzatto doesn't own the house, she lives in it rent-free, either till her dying day or the demise of the landlord, a generous lover, who shuttles among his homes in various countries, sending postcards to his paramours.

The suitcase disappears into the bedroom, and Grandma requests that her granddaughter take a bath before dinner.

This bathroom is large, it derives from an ancient bathhouse whose remnants include two marble columns and an eagle with one wing, overlooking a deep, narrow bath, from which a twisted copper pipe appears to lead nowhere. But apart from the ancient bath that the architect clearly left intact, all the other appurtenances—faucets and showerheads, sprinklers and handles, soap pumps and towel racks—are totally up to date. For when the landlord comes to visit his house, he regularly brings with him the trendiest hardware, acquired at design shows in Milan or Munich.

"Get undressed, dear, and I'll wash your back."

"No need, I can wash it myself."

"Nobody can do a good soapy back by themselves, there's always a spot that cannot be reached, so let's go, young lady."

"Who soaps that spot on your back?"

"Someone..."

"Who?"

"Maybe you'll meet him tomorrow night," Grandma laughs, "but meanwhile let's get moving."

Quickly but gently, Grandma peels off her granddaughter's clothes, turns on the three showerheads, adjusts the temperature, and with a large loofa scrubs not only her back, but her young breasts, long legs and plump white backside, then she washes her hair with aromatic shampoo, not omitting her golden, downy pubic hair. But Grandma, I'm not a baby, you don't need to wash me. You're not a baby, but soon enough there won't be anyone around to make sure you're properly washed, so close your eyes and turn over. She raises the water pressure and thoroughly cleanses the young body, and only once she's sure the last soap bubble has vanished, she wraps her granddaughter in a warm bathrobe and hugs her close.

"Your father told me on the phone that the old Nazi decided you look like me."

Yes, whispers Rachele, but he also said you were more beautiful. I really was beautiful, and no doubt that was why he was willing to deliver your father, but don't worry, dear, you'll be beautiful enough to find a husband who will take better care of you than your father takes of your mother.

* * *

Dinner is served by a silent Ethiopian woman with a bird tattooed on her forehead. Where are Claudia and Camilla and Lucia, and Maxim and Mauro, all the people who work for you? I shipped them off to their children and grandchildren for Christmas. The hospital sent an Ethiopian family to help me out. An entire family? How many are they? I didn't count them, but the house is big enough, and they're not fussy. Why did they come here on Christmas? Papà says the Ethiopians are also Christians. True, there are Ethiopian Christians, and Ethiopian Muslims, and even, believe it or not, Ethiopian Jews. I heard that Israel suddenly remembered them and brought them over, instead of European Jews who don't want to move to Israel. But the Ethiopians who were sent to me are not Christians or Muslims or Jews, but Ethiopians who believe in spirits and stars, and their holidays are apparently at a different time of year. But how do you communicate with them? Do they speak Italian? It's hard to understand them, just as it was hard for your father to understand the Tyrolean teacher. What can you do, everyone concocts his or her own Italian at will. But I don't have to understand these Ethiopians, they need to understand me, and if even one of them guesses what I want, the whole family will understand and do as I ask.

✳ ✳ ✳

After dinner she finds an Ethiopian girl of her own age in her bedroom, unpacking her suitcase, folding and hanging, diligently putting each item where it belongs. When Rachele gets in bed the Ethiopian hurries to place a hot water bottle at her feet, and covers her with a blanket. But as she slides the empty suitcase under the bed, she realizes that something was left in it, and she pulls it back out and retrieves the *Heart*, leafs through it and looks at the illustrations, then gently lays the book by Rachele's head, turns all the lights off and leaves.

Venice rustles in the deep velvety darkness: the sighing of water in the canals, the jostling of boats, the strong gusty winds skating down from the Alps.

12

The next morning, awaiting the grandmother and granddaughter at a shop in the southern arcade of Piazza San Marco, is Lucja the seamstress, a Polish woman of sixty or so, who will help them decide which of the three dresses Grandma selected yesterday is best for the party. But since Grandma is prepared to buy all three, and indeed has already paid for them, and also for a fourth she chose at the last minute, the final decision will come only this evening, and in the meantime the expert seamstress will try to alter all four. Rachele goes in and out of the fitting room, under the professional eye of the proprietor, who offers his opinion. And because the purpose of trying them on is not to decide which to wear but basic tailoring, the seamstress's kit includes not only pins and needles and thread and a tape measure but a wealth of decorative addenda: beads, lace ribbons, gilded pins, all manner of buttons old and new. All these are meant to add unique touches to the rather spartan dresses chosen in advance by Grandma.

Rachele is patient, doesn't argue. Goes in, tries on, comes out, stands again and again in front of the three mirrors, giving herself over to the creative imagination of the seamstress, who is now alone with Rachele, since Grandma has gone off to find a dress for herself. Lucja, whom Grandma insists on calling Miriam, undoes the hems of the four dresses so they cover the girl's bony knees, which bear scratches from athletic ventures the energetic father imposed on his daughter. At your age, explains the seamstress, girls' knees are not yet interesting to boys, shapely calves are the thing, which is why Grandma got you high-heeled shoes. I will never wear heels, declares Rachele, so many boys in my class at school are shorter than me, and I don't want to be taller still. Go argue with your Grandma, the seamstress interrupts, I specialize in dresses, not shoes. But how, Rachele challenges her, can you accept Grandma changing your name from Lucja to Miriam? I don't like to argue with generous people who pay double what others do. And why did she choose Miriam? Because if I came to Italy as a child, she said, I must be a little bit Jewish. A little bit? Rachele laughs, How little? Why only a little? I don't know, blushes the seamstress, but I agreed to this "little bit" only on condition that I can eat anything I want and in what order, and also, if you happen to have another Holocaust, I won't have to participate.

Grandma storms into the changing room, quickly undresses, and slips into a long black velvet dress. Her body is tall, statuesque, even as her age is apparent in her wrinkled skin and drooping breasts. Lucja-Miriam kneels down to mark the hem. The top of the ankle, warns the grandmother, not a millimeter more. The proprietor sneaks a look: Perfect, Signora Luzzatto, perfect, no need to add a thing.

"But I have a gorgeous pendant," protests the seamstress, "an antique made of silver to enhance the beauty of the black velvet."

"We'll consider that, put it in with the rest, thank you, Miriam, we'll try everything at home. And after she instructs the store owner where to send the packages, and slides an envelope to the seamstress, the two cross the piazza to buy the granddaughter a mask. Mask? wonders

Rachele, why? Carnival isn't for another month, and it's not a Jewish holiday. True, Carnival isn't our holiday, Grandma says, nor are the guests this evening looking for a carnival but rather culture and history, so they'll be wearing masks, my party is also a masquerade."

"Jewish people?"

"Jewish and non-Jewish, including the director of the hospital who helped your father understand his illness."

"Is he Jewish?"

"A little bit . . ."

"What's a little bit? Like Lucja?"

"No, because he once had a Jewish wife, and ever since he's been a little bit Jewish. When your father told him about you, he said he wanted to meet you."

"Meet me? Why?"

"He'll explain."

"Wait," Rachele asks anxiously, "will there be anyone like me, I mean, my age?"

"No, only you. And you can go to bed whenever you like. You won't hear a sound in your room."

"But why," Rachele persists, "why did you tell Lucja that she's a little bit Jewish, and why did you change her name?"

Grandma is amused. Because Lucja is like Jews who bring an extra something to the goyim, like adding buttons or epaulets, or colorful velvet collars.

"Like Papà, you say 'goyim,' not Christians or Catholics,

and that is an insult to me, because you're calling my other grandparents goyim."

"Wonderful and refined goyim, and I will hug them with much love at the synagogue when I see them at your bat mitzvah."

They enter the mask shop, which seems small, with a limited inventory. But it turns out that steep stairs lead to a large sealed-off cellar, with the waters of the canal slapping the outside wall. And since Grandma will wear the same mask tonight as last year, only Rachele needs to choose one. In the dim light they survey big masks and small, simple and sophisticated, realistic and fantastical, historical and contemporary, and Grandma points to one or another and says, this is wonderful, this is unique, this one is funny, this one is scary, I've never seen one like it. But Rachele doesn't respond, or pick up any mask to try on in front of the small mirrors. Deeply serious, she walks down the aisles in stony silence, half-listening to her grandmother, who now and then can't resist trying on a mask, delighting in her amazing changes of character.

"So, young lady, make up your mind, it's only a mask, after all."

Rachele points to a mask on an upper shelf. The smiling face of a young Jew, wearing a big kippah, its greenish glass eyes twinkling, golden sidelocks dangling from its ears.

"This Jewboy? But it's a man's face, a young man."

"Why does that matter?" grumbles Rachele. "It's only a mask, after all."

With a hook-ended stick a shop assistant takes the Jew down from the shelf, shakes dust from its sidelocks and primps the curls. Wait, he announces, we also have a little hat for him.

Rachele puts on the mask. I can't see a thing, she says, why the eyes? The glass is quite transparent, apologizes the salesman, you can see through it, but if you want to get rid of the eyes, no problem, just push them, they'll pop loose.

Facing her bedroom mirror, Rachele puts the mask on and tries to see the world through greenish glass, but everything is blurry and distorted. Without thinking twice she pokes out the eyes and two little spheres drop to the floor and roll under the bed. After applying a touch of red lipstick to the yeshiva boy's cheeks, she again dons the mask and goes to introduce her character to the Ethiopians preparing the house for the party. While they may not entirely grasp the new look of the Signora's granddaughter, they're happy to see the first mask wandering through the house.

* * *

Rachele closes her bedroom door for her afternoon nap, but the new dresses silently hung on the closet door have infiltrated her room while she slept. Can a Jew with blond *payess* go with one of the dresses? Won't it be seen as frivolous contempt for religion and identity? Grandma agrees, so early in the evening Rachele won't wear a dress but will show up in black gym clothes and the mask, as if the yeshiva boy had just returned from exercising. Only later, when other guests have shed their masks to enjoy the food, will Rachele go to her room and reappear in her new dress.

At around nine the first costumed guests arrive, observing a code of silence to obscure their identities. Everyone is amazed by a woman (or a man?) dressed like a Taliban housewife. She is wrapped in several layers of clothing, transmuted into an opaque tent that seems to lack pinholes to let her see or breathe, and she drifts, without tripping or stumbling, from room to room of the big house, as if governed by an internal radar. In addition to this exciting but frightening costume, most of the rest are inspired by politics or popular culture, and some by Venetian history, which boasts many eminences worth remembering as the new year begins. And because most of the guests guess that the yeshiva boy, standing in a corner in gym clothes, twirling his sidelocks, is also the beloved only grandchild of the hostess, they lavish hugs and praises upon him.

Inevitably late, at nearly ten o'clock, arrives the successor of Claudio Monteverdi, Francesco Cavalli, a Venetian composer and organist who died three centuries ago, and is portrayed tonight by the director of the local hospital, Salvatore Novarese, himself a beloved and admired figure. And because the assembled know that sooner or later they will need his medical care, they cheer him roundly, extolling his elaborate costume, and someone hums an aria by the composer. But the hospital director, taking the arm of the hostess, asks to be introduced without delay to the daughter of Riccardo Luzzatto, who came to him a few days earlier for tests and will return to the hospital after the holiday.

"Here she is," says the grandmother, pointing at the young Talmud scholar, "here's our Rachele."

The hospital director is impressed by the costume, and palpates one of the *payess* with two fingers, and then, at Grandma's request, Rachele takes off the mask and hat, shakes out her curls, and gazes at the physician, who seems to exude, though disguised as a classical composer, an aroma of medicines.

"So you are Riccardo's daughter?"

"Yes."

"And your name?"

"Rachele."

"You have a brother or sister?"

"No, I'm an only child."

"Your grandfather told me he tacks your lovely school compositions to his bulletin board."

"He likes doing that."

"How old are you?"

"Soon Rachele will be twelve," says the grandmother, "and we'll celebrate her bat mitzvah."

"What is a bat mitzvah?" inquires the hospital director, and Grandma explains.

"You know about your father's illness? He told you?"

"Yes," Rachele whispers. "You found an appendage in his brain."

"Appendage?"

"That's how he explained it."

"Everyone says you're a bright girl, but now you need to be not just bright but strong."

"Right."

"You'll have to be strong, like other children."

"Which children?"

"Ask your teacher about children who stayed strong."

"Strong how?"

The heart of the seventeenth-century composer goes out

to the girl who holds in her hand the face of a frail yeshiva boy, and he reaches for her head as if to examine it. Then he withdraws and walks to the buffet, encircled by Ethiopians.

"No, don't put the mask back on," Grandma tells her. "Go to your room and pick out one of the dresses, add a little color to your cheeks, and come back and taste the endless wonderful food. You've barely eaten since this morning."

Rachele returns to her room, strips off the gym clothes, considers the choice of dresses, and is suddenly terrified. In her underwear, she turns off the light and curls up under the thick blanket, as if hoping the warmth will dispel her anxiety. Indeed, no sounds of the party are audible here. She remembers the copy of *Cuore* that the Ethiopian girl placed last evening by her bed, gropes for the book, takes it under the blanket, and kisses it in the darkness, thinking about her teacher Emilia Gironi, who asked her not only to read the story that was cut off midway but to choose another story and compare the two. She switches on the night light, turns pages, and comes upon "The Little Florentine Scribe," about the boy who stays up all night copying addresses, to assist his father.

> Nevertheless he rose that night, more by force of habit than anything else; and since he was up, he wanted to go and see once again, for the last time,

in the quiet of the night, the little chamber where
he toiled in secret with his heart full of satisfaction
and tenderness. And when he beheld that little
table with the lamp lighted and those white
envelopes on which he was nevermore to write the
names of persons and towns he had come to know
by heart, he was seized with a great sadness, and
impetuously he grasped the pen to return to his
accustomed toil. But in reaching out his hand he
struck a book, and the book fell. His heart skipped
a beat. What if his father had woken! Certainly he
would not have discovered him committing a bad
deed: he had himself decided to tell him all, and yet
the sound of that step approaching in the darkness,
the discovery at that hour, in that silence, his
mother, who would be awakened and alarmed, and
the thought that his father might feel humiliated
on thus discovering all, terrified him. He bent his
ear, with suspended breath. He heard no sound.
He laid his ear to the lock of the door behind him;
nothing. The whole house was asleep. He recovered
his composure, and he set himself again to his
writing, and envelope was piled on envelope. He
heard the regular tread of the policeman below in
the deserted street; then the rumble of a carriage
which gradually died away; then, after an interval,

the rattle of a file of carts, which passed slowly by; then a profound silence, broken from time to time by the distant barking of a dog. And he wrote on and on: and meanwhile his father was behind him. He had risen on hearing the book fall, and had remained waiting for a long time: the rattle of the carts had drowned his footsteps and the creaking of the doorcase; and he stood there, his white head bent over Giulio's little black head, and he had seen the pen flying over the envelopes, and in an instant he had divined all, understood all, and a desperate regret, but at the same time an immense tenderness, had taken possession of his mind and nailed him to the spot behind his child. Suddenly Giulio uttered a piercing shriek: two trembling arms had enfolded his head.

"Oh, Papà, Papà! Forgive me, forgive me!" he cried, recognizing his parent.

"You, forgive me!" replied his father, sobbing, and covering the boy's forehead with kisses. "I have understood everything, I know everything; it is I, it is I who ask your forgiveness, my blessed little creature; come, come with me!"

13

Salvatore Novarese isn't just content to portray Francesco Cavalli, he wants to showcase his music too, so he sits down at the piano and begins to play a canzone by the Baroque composer, to prove to his friends that despite the burdens of his profession, he is also an expert in the oeuvre of his seventeenth-century lookalike. The guests are therefore compelled to wait patiently for the professor to exhaust his musical passion before seizing the opportunity, one by one, to pepper him with personal medical queries.

And so, amid a counterpoint of piano music and medical research, the cultural and educational evening passes pleasantly, and as midnight approaches, the guests take leave of their hostess and each other with kisses and wishes of good health for the new year, two days hence. But the Grandma, still holding a crystal goblet of red wine, as on any given day by sundown, is in no hurry to go to bed. She wants to restore order in her chaotic house, and directs the senior Ethiopian, napping between pots and pans, to rally his people. Ethiopians large and small emerge from every corner of the big house, first gathering abandoned masks and stashing them in a large bag, then clearing plates and glasses, collecting tablecloths, and piling chairs on top of tables so they can sweep and wash the floors.

Meanwhile the Grandma is trying to recall, in her foggy inebriation, if any of the dresses acquired in Piazza San Marco had popped up among the guests or remained an unfulfilled wish. And as tablecloths and napkins whirl in the washing machine, she is horrified by the strange notion that her granddaughter, thrilled by the mask she chose, has escaped among the canals, to mystify the residents of Venice as a Jew with sidelocks, in flight from the Old Ghetto. She rushes at once to her room, where four dresses hover over the yeshiva boy lying on the floor beside the open *Heart*. What happened? The Grandma pulls the blanket and holds her granddaughter tight. Why did you run away from the party? And the girl's anger bursts through fragments of a dream, directed at the man who demanded, without showing his face, that she be strong and keep a stiff upper lip.

And the Grandma, realizing how deeply the hospital director had rattled her granddaughter, tries to calm her down. "Yes, it was a mistake on his part to demand that you be strong, because everyone who knows you knows how strong you are. But your mask may have misled him into thinking that you are a Jewish weakling, and not a tough, bright girl."

Rachele gradually calms down, realizing she had gone to bed hungry, and asks if any delicacies are left over from the party. Yes, a wide selection awaits Rachele in the kitchen, but because the cleaners are on the job, it's best that Grandma put together a plate for her. Very good, says Rachele, but be careful, Grandma, not to bring me anything with meat. What's wrong with meat? Depends which meat. We girls in Hebrew class promised our teacher, Rabbi Azoulay, that at least until bat mitzvah we'll keep kosher, and you, Grandma, even though you're a Jew the Germans wanted to kill, will never be able to tell the difference between kosher and non-kosher, not that it's easy to tell, in Italy even in a simple bread roll they sometimes use lard. Pig fat in a bread roll? The Grandma is shocked. Why? So it will taste better, that's what the rabbi said.

Grandma laughs. You have an odd rabbi, if he knows the taste of a roll he never ate. No, he's not odd, just curious, and he was sent to Italy because they couldn't find him a bride in Jerusalem. But he's a nice rabbi and not too strict; for example, he doesn't care that Sabrina, who gets Christianized day after day by the nuns of Sacred Heart, is also in our Hebrew class.

"But what happens after your bat mitzvah?" teases Grandma. "Will the rabbi then permit the girls to eat rolls with pig fat?" After bat mitzvah each girl will decide according to her conscience, replies Rachele in a democratic spirit. And you, dear, what will you decide? For now I'm still thinking, haven't yet decided. In that case, concludes the Grandma, put on a robe and go to the kitchen and decide for yourself what's yummy and also kosher.

And the Ethiopians, done with their labors but still uncertain if they may now go to bed, watch with curiosity as the girl surveys the delicacies. Though they fail to understand her logic, Rachele piles all the meaty treats on a tray, and presents it to them.

* * *

When she returns to her room with the food, she finds Grandma in her bed, fast asleep, with *Cuore* lying close to her heart. Rachele is careful not to wake her. She rests the tray on her lap and eats cheeses, pasta shells filled with ricotta and spinach, tiny reddish pizzas, almond cookies crispy on the outside and soft within, and while eating studies the sleeper's face, whose makeup, which shone earlier in the evening, has turned into ugly gray patches, the smiles she generously bestowed on her guests have deepened her wrinkles at this hour of night. If everyone says I resemble my Jewish Grandma, Rachele sadly thinks, and not my Nonna who believes in nothing, I'll end up wrinkled like her, even though she was once beautiful. And while she considers whether she has an appetite for another trayful, her Grandma opens her eyes and commends the width of the bed, which came from the old maternity hospital of Venice, where it was customary to place the baby beside the mother, not in a separate crib. It's apparently because of this wonderful bed that her houseguests extend their stay. But why does a girl in middle school still read a childish book like *Cuore*?

"Yes, it's childish," agrees Rachele, "and we read it in elementary school. But our old teacher, who was about to retire, decided in honor of Christmas to read us stories from

Cuore, so we would become, in her words, more human in the new year."

"More human in the new year?" Grandma is impressed. "That's lovely. And that's why you're reading this book now?"

"Not because of the humanity but because of the teacher. While she was reading us the story called 'Daddy's Nurse,' a student from an upper grade came to tell me not to go home but rather to Grandpa's office, since Papà was still in Venice for tests at the hospital. And then the teacher, who always liked me, asked that I finish the story on my own and read one more, and during vacation to come to her house and tell her what I think about both stories."

"And you'll really do it?"

"No way. Why would I? She won't be teaching us anymore, what do I have to say to her? Even though she really did like me."

"How do you know?"

"Because she always called on me when I raised my hand, and if she was talking and I happened to raise my hand, she would stop and let me talk. And you know, she tied a silk ribbon to my wrist, so I'd remember to visit her."

"Really? Show me."

"Here, I still have it," says Rachele, displaying her wrist.

"No, don't remove it, dear. Go visit her."

"But why? She won't be teaching us anymore."

"That doesn't matter. If she likes you, go talk to her about the stories you read. Don't disappoint her."

"But how will I ever find her?"

"What's her name?"

"Emilia."

"Emilia what?"

"Emilia Gironi."

"I'll find her for you, and you'll go visit her, and ask her to tell you about students with parents who were sick but they knew how to stay strong."

"And the stories? What do I tell her?"

"Finish the second one, and think about what it has in common with 'Daddy's Nurse,' and how they differ from each other."

"That's not easy."

"There's always something to say about stories."

"But how'll you be able to find her?"

"I'll find her for you."

"And what will I get out of it?"

"There's always something to be learned from an elderly teacher."

"But be careful, Grandma, if you happen to find her, don't make her any promises in my name. Only I will decide whether or not to visit her."

"Fine. I won't promise anything before you give me permission to do so. Now allow me to cover you, and it's good you left your socks on, if the blanket falls off during the night you'll still be warm."

"Just a minute, Grandma, another thing. Don't be surprised if you discover that the meat goodies you left in the kitchen have disappeared."

"How did they disappear?"

"I gave them to your Ethiopians."

"The Ethiopians? Why?"

"You said that these Ethiopians aren't Christians or Muslims, and that the Ethiopian Jews were moved to Israel, it means the only ones remaining to help you are Ethiopians who believe in spirits and stars, and spirits and stars don't care what is kosher and what isn't."

"The rabbi from Jerusalem has driven you crazy," laughs the Grandma, turns out the light, and leaves.

But Rachele puts the light back on to finish "The Little Florentine Scribe":

> And he pushed or rather carried him to the bedside of his mother, who was awake, and casting him into her arms, he said:
>
> "Kiss this little angel of a son, who has not slept for three months, but has been toiling for me, while I was saddening his heart, and he was earning our bread!" The mother pressed him to her breast and held him there, unable to collect her thoughts; at

last she said: "Go to sleep at once, my baby, go to sleep and rest. Carry him to bed."

The father took him from her arms, carried him to his room, and laid him in his bed, and still breathing hard and caressing him, arranged his pillows and blankets for him.

"Thank you, Papà," the child kept repeating; "thanks; but go to bed yourself now; I am content; go to bed, Papà."

But his father wanted to see him fall asleep; so he sat down by the bed, took his hand, and said to him, "Sleep, sleep, my little son!" and Giulio, exhausted, fell asleep at last, and slumbered many hours, enjoying, for the first time in many months, a tranquil sleep, enlivened by pleasant dreams. And as he opened his eyes, when the sun had already been shining for some time, he first felt, and then saw, close to his breast, and resting upon the edge of the little bed, the white head of his father, who had passed the night thus, and who was still asleep, with his brow against his son's heart.

14

And Rachele in Venice, enjoying unlimited slumber, joins the reconciled father and son sleeping sweetly in Florence. And only in late morning the grandmother leans over her young double, to tell her that Papà had decided to skip the New Year's party at the hotel in Cortina, and that Paolo will soon be on his way to the Dolomites to pick up her parents from the hotel, not to take them home but to bring them here to Venice. If your father is willing to forgo the party at the hotel—certainly, he wore himself out—I suggested he rest here before going home. Very good, Rachele agrees, I'll let him have the childbirth bed so he can sleep as soundly as I did last night, and you can find me another one.

"But not here."

"Not here? Where?"

"I found your teacher, dear, and she really loves you very much. She was so happy to hear that you'll come to see her."

"What? You found her so fast? And you promised I'd go there? Why? I told you not to say anything until I decide if I really want to see her."

"But Rachele, she's a dear teacher who was so happy when I told her you wanted to come visit."

"She can be as happy as she likes, but I won't be happy to visit her."

"Why?"

"Because as I explained to you, she's an old lady who will not be teaching me anymore."

"Why do you keep calling her old? I'm older than she is. Even if she won't be your teacher, she can advise you how to behave when Papà is in the hospital."

"I don't understand how you found her so quickly."

"I called your principal and she gave me the phone number and address, she also said Signora Gironi would not be teaching you anymore."

"That's exactly what I said. So what's in it for me if I visit her?"

"What do you mean, 'what's in it for me?' That's not nice, what a petty thought. Just go talk with her, you're a serious and thoughtful girl, you'll learn from her, and she from you."

"What can she learn from me?"

"One always learns something from everyone, just as I learned from you things I didn't know about the Jews, about the rabbi who's looking for a bride in Italy and knows about bread rolls with pig fat. Come, my dearest girl, come, sweetheart, get up, get dressed, eat breakfast and be ready to go."

"Go where?"

"To your teacher."

"Now? Today? Why the rush?"

"Because Signora Gironi is traveling tomorrow to her sister in Sicily, and by the time she returns, you won't remember her, or anything about the stories you read."

"So Papà and Mamma will stay and sleep here, and you want me to go and come back? Because I won't sleep at our house if there's no one else there."

"You don't have to come back here, or sleep alone. I spoke to Nonno Ernesto, and he'll pick you up, and at night you'll be with your other Grandma, whom you love so much, and talk to the parrot who is waiting for you at her house."

"I can't believe it." Rachele burst into tears of rage. "You arranged everything, you looked into everything, even the parrot they gave me as a present. Why? What did I do to you? Why the hurry? I told you that I am the one to decide about visiting an old teacher who will not teach me anymore . . . Why, while I sleep innocently, do you turn my life upside down?"

"Not upside down. I make it stronger."

"Again, stronger? All the time, stronger. How so? Just yesterday you said that I'm strong enough."

"You're very strong, but it's always possible to be stronger. And why are you crying? Papà will be pleased that you're visiting a teacher who loves you and believes in you."

"How do you know that Papà will be pleased?"

"Because I gave birth to him. You even went into the mountains to see where I gave birth."

"So what if you gave birth to him?"

"That's why I know what he feels and what he wants."

And at three o'clock in the afternoon the gondola booked by Paolo is tied to a post behind Grandma's kitchen. The deaf and mute gondolier extends his arms to receive the girl handed over by an old Ethiopian. The gondolier carefully seats her in the front, and though she is wearing a coat, he covers her with a thick fur blanket. And when the Ethiopian, as the girl's escort, climbs into the gondola behind her, it appears as if the boat might tip over, but the grandmother quickly unties the rope connecting the gondola to her house, and the gondolier drops the long oar deep into the foul water to steady it. This time in silence, without old music or new tunes, the black gondola makes its way through the canals, till the bow bumps the dock of the railway station.

Despite the clear sky the Ethiopian opens an umbrella over the girl's head, and buys her a one-way ticket to her native city and a round-trip ticket for himself. After he wedges Rachele's bag into the overhead baggage rack, the Ethiopian pulls a slip of paper from his pocket listing the stations on the train route, with the last one in red ink and big letters.

Rachele has taken this train quite a few times, and she'll know when she arrives in her hometown, but she sits and says nothing, so as not to burden her chaperon. He's a sturdy fellow of her father's age, and his gray hair adds a touch of majesty to his dark face. If he were less focused on the stations they pass, she might ask him to explain the nature of the god of the spirits and what he demands of his adherents, but she suspects his limited knowledge of Italian would trip him up and confuse her, and his mind is focused on the mission he has been assigned. Indeed, as soon as the train leaves the station prior to hers, he stands, hoists her bag on his shoulder, and gives the girl a look, a polite reminder to get ready.

❊ ❊ ❊

On the way to the taxi stand he holds in his hand the teacher's address, and under clear skies he again shields the girl with the umbrella, perhaps against some hidden spirit that he alone can sense. The taxi driver is doubtless asking himself whether the beautiful girl whom the Ethiopian put in the back seat has been kidnapped, so Rachele is quick to reassure him, speaking softly in dialect, don't worry, sir, we're only going to visit an old teacher of mine to wish her a happy New Year. And peering from afar, from an unexpected direction, are the three towers of the cathedral, whose name Rachele will now remember forever.

The Ethiopian, however, isn't satisfied merely to locate the building, he escorts the girl to the third floor, and before ringing the doorbell to confirm the success of his mission, he double-checks that the name on the door is the same as the one written on the piece of paper. But because the Grandma forgot to warn Signora Gironi that her student would arrive accompanied, the teacher opens the door in a simple dress, her hair unkempt. She is taken aback at the sight of a big African man plotting to invade her home, and might have slammed the door in his face had not Rachele darted from behind to calm her teacher, no, Signora, this is someone who accompanied me on the trip here.

The teacher Emilia appears more youthful in her apartment, which is small and old, and the Ethiopian, although aware his errand is accomplished, hesitates. In another minute he'd surely be invited to taste the panettone dominating the small living room, but he decides it's time to go, bows his head in a farewell gesture of thanks but also of refusal, and in precise Italian explains to the teacher that Rachele's parents will soon arrive in Venice and he is hurrying back to help them settle in. Then he remembers the bag, removes it from his shoulder, sets it down by the door, and leaves.

"Your grandmother took on an African helper?" She is intrigued.

"No, he belongs to the hospital. Her whole staff is off for the holidays, so she got him from the hospital director for the New Year celebrations."

"And what's his name?"

"How should I know?"

"You rode with him on the train for an hour and didn't ask his name?"

"I didn't know if he'd understand the question."

"But you just heard that he understands and speaks."

"True, and it's really too bad that I didn't talk to him, not to find out his name, but because according to Grandma, he's the type of Ethiopian whose god doesn't hide far away in the sky, like ours, the Jews and Christians. Their god floats close to earth, with the winds, and he might have explained to me how that works."

The teacher looks at her student with a smile. Yes, in the Teachers' Room they were saying that you always have God on your mind, which is why they wanted you to be the Mother of God in the play, but your father wouldn't allow it.

"Because he thought I would confuse acting with praying. Do you too think it's possible to confuse them?"

"That depends upon the actor," says the teacher, "only the actor."

And she cuts a thick slice off the panettone, and offers to crown it with mascarpone. How did you know I like cream on my cake? Rachele is surprised. Because I saw you in the pastry shop asking for it. The *pasticceria*? Rachele is shocked. Which one? On Garibaldi, near school. Strange, mumbles Rachele, I didn't see you there. Not important, dear, it doesn't matter, the main thing is that you finished reading the story on your own, and that you came to tell me what you think of it, compared to 'The Little Florentine Scribe.'"

"Wait a minute, how do you know that the story I chose is 'The Little Florentine Scribe?'"

"Your grandmother told me, and she read it too, while you were sleeping, and even cried a little at the end." She cried over the little scribe? My Grandma? I can't believe it. I never thought she was capable of crying over anybody. Well, there you are, Rachele, this time your Grandma did cry, which is why she wanted so much for you to visit an old teacher like me, who will not teach you anymore, so you can tell me your impressions of the stories. She also asked me to talk to you about something else.

Rachele is silent, thinks a while, then eyes the teacher and says:

"Fine, if it's really important to you to know what I think, in my opinion 'Daddy's Nurse' is a much better story than 'The Little Florentine Scribe.'"

"Why?"

"Because it's true that Cicillo mistakenly thought the sick man was his father, but that wasn't his fault alone. The nurses and doctors could have pointed out his error, but they were negligent. And if everyone thought he took care of the stranger only because he thought the man was his father, we see it's not so. Even when the real, healthy father arrived, smothering him in hugs and kisses, and he understood that the dying patient was not his father, he asked permission to stay with him. And his own father actually gave his permission, and the doctors also praised him that, instead of going home to the village with his father to celebrate his recovery, he stayed in the hospital with a dying man he didn't know. That's why I really liked Cicillo in this story, and by the way, Signora Emilia, you were wrong, the student sent by the principal to fetch me in the middle of a lesson was called not Cicillo but Emilio."

"Yes, I know, my dear. But sometimes I intentionally attach the names of the fictional protagonists to my students, so they'll feel that the characters in the stories are as real as they are. Would you like another piece of cake?"

"Maybe later."

"But why didn't you like Giulio, the little scribe?"

"Because he tricked his father and got him in trouble."

"In trouble? He was helping him."

"But he didn't get permission from his father. And because he was up at night working, he did poorly at school, which pained his father very much."

"But if he wanted to help his father, who was clearly having a hard time, how else could he have helped him?"

"Very simple. He could have said to him: Papà, I'll help you, and after finishing his homework, he would sit down and work for one hour in the evening, addressing the envelopes. That way it's with permission and without deception."

"But perhaps he was afraid that his father wouldn't agree. That his father would feel humiliated to have his son work in his place."

"That's the father's problem, not Giulio's. His handwriting was similar to his father's. So the father should have agreed. But he didn't suggest it to his father, he just got up night after night, and if he hadn't accidentally dropped the book, his father would have kept on sleeping, and never realized that his son was doing his work for him, and kept on thinking he was a success and his son a failure."

"That's what you thought when you read the story?"

"That's what I think now too. It's good that the book fell down in the middle of the night and the father caught Giulio. Because Giulio was not okay, and my Grandma should not have cried for him, if in fact she did."

Signora Emilia regards her excited student with a little smile.

"Nice. You know how to think."

Rachele blushes. "I try," she says. "It's not always easy."

"I know," the teacher agrees. "You want another slice of cake now?"

"A little one."

"Again with mascarpone?"

"If possible."

And the teacher garnishes the slice with the white cream and says gently: "Grandma told me your father is a bit ill."

"Yes, they found a kind of appendage in his head."

"Appendage?"

"That's what I call it, in other words, something extra."

"Like Andrea's father."

"Which Andrea?"

"The boy in the seat closest to the door."

"Andrea Bolzano?"

"Right, Bolzano."

"He never spoke about his father."

"He's a strong boy who doesn't complain. His mother sits long hours at the hospital, and he picks up his little brother from kindergarten and brings him home and looks after him. The mother of Enrico, who was sent to take you from the lesson, has also been very ill, for more than a year now. He didn't tell you anything?"

"The student you called Cicillo?"

"Yes."

"He didn't tell me a thing. He actually seemed like one of those happy and contented people."

"Because he knows how to overcome his fear and sadness. He also didn't ask for any special favors at school. He wasn't late or careless, always did his homework.

His teacher is very impressed. I had many such students during my many years of teaching. Students we teachers knew were facing hard times at home, but nevertheless bore up bravely."

"Even those who in the end turned into orphans?"

"Yes, dear, there are even some of those."

The rays of the setting sun caress the cream on the slice of cake, and Rachele bores through the white mound into the golden brown, feeling grateful to the teacher who has surrounded her with strong students who don't despair even though their parents are sick or dead. Then there is the loud, hoarse ring of an old telephone, and the teacher picks up the receiver.

"It's your Grandpa. He wants to talk to you."

Grandpa Ernesto's voice sounds muffled and remote as he asks about the visit to the teacher. Everything's fine, Nonno, I'm telling Signora Emilia what I think about the stories in *Cuore*, the book that Nonna bought for me.

It turns out that Nonno and Nonna are still with Nonna's sister in Venice, waiting for other guests from a nearby village to join them for dinner, so Ernesto wants to know if Rachele could wait another two and a half hours to be picked up, or would she rather they skip the dinner and come get her now. Another two and a half hours? Rachele is caught off guard. So late? What'll I do in the meantime? But her grandpa doesn't give up easily, dinner with old friends who take the trouble to come from the village appeals to him greatly, and he would like to know if Signora Gironi could entertain her student for two more hours.

"Tell them," says Signora Gironi, "that as far as I'm concerned they can get here whenever they want, and you can stay here as long as you like, we have plenty to talk about, after all."

"It won't be late for you?"

"No, I go to bed late, but maybe you'll be tired."

"Yes, I'm already tired."

"If so, maybe just sleep here, and that way your grandparents will have more time to spend with their friends."

"Sleep here?" Rachele is unnerved. "How? There's enough room?"

"Of course. Let me talk to your Grandpa."

Nonno and Nonna are very pleased by the offer. This way they won't be under pressure. Rachele has pajamas and underwear and toiletries in her pack. If she agrees to stay, they will be grateful to Signora Gironi.

"What about the parrot?" asks Rachele.

"He won't run away. He'll be there waiting for you tomorrow."

Rachele surveys the small apartment with concern. She really hadn't wanted to come even for a short visit, and now she has been forced to sleep here. Yet now she's somewhat attracted to the teacher's modest apartment, so different from the large apartments of her family and relatives.

The teacher shows her student the room that had been her daughter's before she moved to England. It is small, like the rest of the rooms in the flat. It is tidy and clean, and the bed is wide, covered with a flowered spread. On the wall overhead is a large painting. A golden-haired youth climbs a mountain alone, facing the sunrise.

"Why did your daughter decide to live in England?"

"She's a single mother, and there, among strangers, nobody cares that her little girl doesn't have a father."

"And you go to visit your granddaughter?"

"Not much, not enough, because I don't speak English, and my granddaughter doesn't understand Italian."

"So why don't you learn English, so you can talk to her?"

"I tried, but Italian runs so deep in me, it drives away every other language."

"Why? I'm learning Hebrew, and my Italian loves it."

"Where are you learning Hebrew?"

"With a rabbi who was sent to us from Jerusalem, to me and other girls like me. Did you know, Signora, that Hebrew is written backwards, from right to left, and the letters are also different? If you want, I can write them for you, or maybe sing you a prayer in Hebrew, so you can get a sense of how it sounds."

"Very good, but on condition that you explain what you're singing."

And Rachele gets up and stands ceremoniously by the window, and facing the twilight begins to sing the prayer intended for her bat mitzvah:

> It is our duty to praise the Lord of all, to ascribe
>   greatness to the author of creation,
> Who has not made us like the nations of the lands,
>   nor placed us like the families of the earth,
> Who has not made our portion like theirs, nor our
>   destiny like all their multitudes.
> For they worship vanity and emptiness, and pray to
>   a god who cannot save.
> But we bow in worship and give thanks unto the
>   Supreme King of kings . . .

The teacher is impressed by the melody and the meter, but can't understand the words. So what does your prayer say, she asks. But Rachele is afraid of upsetting her. Nonno and Nonna are compelled, on account of their Jewish granddaughter, to accept the strange and sometimes cruel prayers of the Jews, but Signora Gironi, who heretofore bore the Jews no grudge and thought of them as unfortunate, might get angry now.

"Not important . . . in other words . . . the prayer says, pretty much, that even if the Jews praise the God who made them different from other people, they are nevertheless like everybody else, in other words, they are human beings."

The teacher detects her uneasiness and makes do without a more faithful translation. She encourages her Jewish student to shower before dinner, and go to bed early. I can tell, dear, that you're tired.

"Not just tired, wiped out."

She is led to a tiny bathroom, also a model of tidiness. And because she is now naked in front of the teacher who will teach her no longer, she senses that it might be this very teacher whom she'll remember more than all the others who will instruct her from now on. As the water douses her body she turns it hotter, and with her eyes closed, imagines Andrea sitting at his desk closest to the door, eagerly awaiting the final bell, so he can hurry to pick up his little brother, who still doesn't know his father will never come back.

✳ ✳ ✳

During dinner the telephone rings again, this time it's Papà in Venice, calling to change the plan for tomorrow. Nonno Ernesto won't pick her up in the morning, it'll be Paolo, who'll drive her to Martina's village, to bring the dog back home. Martina's family think the dog is about to give birth, and don't want to be involved, so it's best that she go home, where the Israeli veterinarian who knows her can assist in the delivery. But why, Rachele wants to know, can't Martina bring her home herself? Because Martina is entitled to celebrate the New Year with her family, not a dog. And because Paolo is reluctant to chauffeur alone a dog who could whelp her litter in his car, he wants you with him, because Diana knows and loves you. If she starts giving birth on the road, she'll feel safe with you by her side.

"But how long is the drive to Martina's village?"

"About an hour and a half."

"In that case I won't have time tomorrow to see the parrot that Nonno bought for me."

"The parrot can wait, he won't run away."

She's wearing her nightie, but before getting under the covers she examines the painting hanging over the bed. Is it a painting or a print? It's a painting my daughter did at the end of high school. Is the boy taken from life, or imaginary? He's imaginary, but not entirely, because she wanted to paint Jesus as he looked at her age. Jesus? Really Jesus? Where? Beside his house, on a hill near Nazareth. She had never been in Nazareth, but she imagined the place, the way painters imagine things. So why did she decide to paint him as a boy, in pictures he's either a baby or grown up and soon to be crucified. Yes, that's exactly why she wanted to paint him as a boy walking alone, with no one at his side. But was he aware in her painting that he was God or the son of God? What did your daughter think when she painted him? I didn't ask her, but even if he already knew that he was God, he didn't want to reveal that to others, so they wouldn't ask him to perform miracles, he wanted to enjoy the freedom and fun of boys his age. If it bothers you, Rachele darling, to sleep with this painting, I'll take it down.

"No, I don't mind if it stays over me, anyway there's almost no chance it's Jesus, and even if it is, he also knows I don't believe in him. But why didn't your daughter take the painting with her to London, why did she leave it here?"

"I asked her to leave it with me. If it keeps you awake let me know, and I'll take it down."

"Don't take it down, I'll be fine."

"It's important that you sleep well, because tomorrow's

going to be a tiring day, traveling to the village to get the dog, what's her name?"

"Diana. She's a hunting dog and not young anymore, so we were surprised to discover she was pregnant."

"I'll help you get cozy. You want me to leave a little light on, or do you prefer the dark?"

"If possible, leave a dim light on, because if I happen to get up in the middle of the night, it'll be hard to get my bearings in an unfamiliar house."

Her fatigue slowly fades. The hills of Galilee? Nazareth? That daughter looked at an Italian mountain and turned it into a Galilee hill. Two years ago, Grandpa and his young wife took Rachele to Israel, and they drove past the hills of Galilee and ate lunch in Nazareth. Did Jesus study in school like everybody else? Or did the Son of God not need to go to school, was there ever a teacher who could teach him anything?

The faint light left on by the teacher seems to be getting stronger, but Rachele is afraid to turn it off. She buries her head in the pillow to fall asleep, but the telephone is again ringing.

"Who was that?" Rachele calls out to her teacher, who stands in the doorway in her nightgown. "I bet it's my Grandma from Venice."

"You guessed right, it's your Grandma, who wanted to know if the Ethiopian man who brought you here told you where he was going."

"Why is she asking?"

"He hasn't come back yet, and she has no idea where he is."

"Maybe the winds took him."

15

The forecasters warned that warm and humid air from the Middle East and cold, dry air from Europe would collide in northern Italy and produce storms and tornadoes. And so, not to have the dog thwart his party plans for New Year's Eve, Paolo decides to leave early for Martina's village. At eight in the morning he is at Signora Emilia's door to rouse the passenger, still enjoying sweet slumber. And Signora Gironi, the old teacher, soon to fly off to her sister in Sicily, shares the driver's concern about country roads that might be blocked, and hurries to feed her houseguest breakfast, the driver as well, and to equip her student with a big, strong umbrella, which Rachele resists, because how and when will she be able to return it to a teacher who will teach her no longer. It is for this very reason the teacher insists that her beloved student borrow an umbrella that can only be returned on another visit, an opportunity to chat about new stories.

"Stories again?"

"There are many stories in the world."

"Again from *Cuore*?"

"No, you're too mature for the *Heart*. Now you should choose stories that trigger thoughts, not tears. Meanwhile, come, I'll hug you, how wonderful that you not only visited me but slept over. And I gather young Jesus didn't disturb you, even if he hovered all night over your head."

"I forgot him the minute I closed my eyes."

In the powerful English car, as the wipers fight the rain that whips the windshield, Paolo has a holiday request for his young passenger. I see that your father has appointed me your permanent driver, so when you grow up, and as an only grandchild you inherit all the property of your rich grandparents, remember me. Even if I'll seem old and weak to you, ask for me and only me to drive you.

"In this car?"

"By then I'll have more cars."

"A high and strong car like this does suit me, but as an Italian I don't like that the dials are on the English side."

"You're right, and that's the first thing I promise to change in the new year, but today don't look at the dashboard but at the map, to make sure I don't get lost, because I decided to get off the highway to Ferrara sooner and take another route, local roads and dirt roads, and that way save at least half an hour in each direction. Please, look at the signs and tell me what they say. I'm focused on the road because of the fog. I don't understand though why your father is so attached to this dog that he won't let her have her puppies in the village."

"It's not my father. Martina's brother is afraid he'll have to supervise an older dog giving birth to purebred puppies that Papà promised to judges and lawyers."

"How many puppies are there in a litter?"

"At her age, no more than three or four."

"How old is she?"

"We got her when she was a puppy, five months old, and I was three, and in two months I'll be twelve, so do the math. She's nine years old plus three months, and it's late for her to give birth, she's near the end of her life."

"When is the end of her life?"

"Maybe twelve or thirteen."

"And how much does each puppy weigh?"

"Two or three hundred grams, depends on the puppy. Some die at birth, that is what Martina's brother is afraid of, he doesn't want to get blamed, these are valuable puppies."

"Tell you the truth, Signorina, it's strange that you have dogs. It doesn't fit right with Jews."

"Depends which Jews you mean, there are Jews and there are Jews. Rabbis, for example, don't have dogs. But my parents couldn't give me a brother, so they gave me a dog."

"And you remained an only child, spoiled and happy."

"Totally not spoiled and not happy. It's sad to be an only child."

"Does the dog have a name?"

"Of course. Diana."

"And what breed is she?"

"Weimaraner. German hunting dog. You know dogs?"

The rain gets stronger, mixing with hailstones. Despite the morning hour, the travelers are swaddled in purple darkness. Fields and villages fade away, leaving only a thick green haze. To improve visibility beyond the frenetic wiper blades, Rachele wipes condensation from inside the windshield with her scarf. Is it wise to veer from the highway to side roads just to save half an hour? But Paolo insists. Now Rachele can make out a sign for Rovigo in three kilometers and warns the driver to slow down, so as not to miss it.

"You're a sharp girl," Paolo compliments her. "One day you'll be like your father and grandfather, who make a fortune helping criminals get out of jail."

"I'm going to be a judge, and I won't allow a fancy speech help anyone go free."

Having abandoned the highway for a maze of country roads, they quickly find themselves on a dirt track, behind a big, slow tractor that ignores their honking and hogs the road, and it's unclear whether the driver can't hear or is just stubborn. So Paolo has no choice but to stop and catch up with the driver on foot. He finds an old farmer behind the wheel wearing earphones that neutralize the engine noise while soothing him with popular arias whose words he knows, not just their melodies. *Signore*, screams Paolo at the tractor driver, some of us are in a hurry. The farmer couldn't imagine that on a stormy day like this, on New Year's Eve, he'd find strangers wandering through the fields. Where're you going in such a hurry? What are you looking for? Paolo tells him the name of Martina's village, and for good measure the tale of the dog.

The farmer shakes his head sadly. You're better off, he advises, to keep following me till the lake up ahead, because if you get stuck there, I am the only one who can rescue you. A lake? Paolo is surprised. There's no lake on the map. It's a winter lake, which disappears in the summer, that's why there is no name on the map. And so they drive behind the tractor on a muddy dirt road and arrive at a lake of sorts, really no more than a winter swamp, apparently not deep, but whatever its depth, the farmer doesn't trust Paolo to cross it. He produces a rope and ties the English car to the tractor and picks up speed across the water until it's impossible to tell whether the car is touching bottom or floating. Even after the fording is over, it's not clear how deep the lake really is. And when it's time to disconnect the vehicles and say goodbye, the farmer warns Paolo, don't you dare try to save time on the way back, because you'll probably get in trouble and end up delivering the puppy dogs all by yourself.

"And maybe nurse them too," jokes Paolo, his spirits lifted by the chance encounter.

16

Paolo congratulates himself on saving at least twenty minutes, despite the unexpected lake. But going home, he adds, we'll take the main road like everyone else. As they approach the village, Rachele opens the window to retrieve a scrap of childhood memory. Ten years ago, on Christmas, when her parents went to Israel with a group of Italian pilgrims, Martina had stayed at their house to look after little Rachele. But on Christmas Eve, her brother arrived and took them both to the village, so Martina could help prepare the big meal and not miss Mass. And in order not to drag the Jewish toddler to a Christian rite they deposited her with an elderly woman in the village. It might have remained a secret, had the child not recalled, several weeks later, the "really yummy" food she was fed in the village. The cook then had no choice but to confess and prepare for the parents the same "really yummy food."

"And this is the dog?" Paolo is astonished by the sight of a spotted pointer greeting the car with savage barking. "She doesn't look like she's about to give birth."

"That's not her," laughs Rachele, "it's her little brother, who looks like her."

From behind one of the houses appears a tall farm woman in overalls and boots, who welcomes the visitors.

In the Luzzatto home, Martina wears a white apron and baker's toque. She serves the food in white gloves, and not a drop of wine strays on its straight path from bottle to glass. Martina excels in baking and desserts, and if Rachele is excited by a dessert at a friend's house, Martina will decipher its recipe and prepare it for the young mistress of the house. But now, in the village, among the fields, Martina is a plump farmer woman, wearing a gray woolen coat, not a trace of white upon her. Good you came early, she says, you'll have time to eat something and rest a bit.

Martina's husband left her many years ago, and when she's in the village she stays with her brother and sister-in-law, the tall peasant woman who had greeted them warmly on arrival. A dog barks in a back room, having sniffed the scent of Rachele, and when the girl hurries to her, she wags her tail energetically but is slow to get up, owing to her pregnancy, to hug her beloved with her front legs. Rachele gets down on her knees and presses the dog's head to her heart. My love, my smart doggie, she says, we're here to take you home.

And while Paolo and Rachele enjoy the multi-course peasants' meal served by Martina, her nephews pad the back seat of the car with old blankets, and as a hail-storm starts rattling the windows, Paolo stands up and says, it's time to go. And since they are taking the main road, the driver doesn't require a navigator at his side, and so Rachele gets into the back seat beside the dog, to calm the animal if need be. It's time to part not only from Martina's family but also from the dog's younger brother, who's not ready to let his sister leave, and he recklessly latches onto the Land Rover and tries to push his way inside, and because he's a dog with no collar, it's hard to control him.

Rachele stretches out alongside the dog, touching her belly and nipples, trying to guess how many puppies she'll give birth to. In honor of the new year Martina has shampooed Diana with the shampoo she herself uses, which makes the dog smell all the more human. If she has a big litter, I can try to persuade Papà to give you one. Me? A German dog? You think I'm crazy? As it is there's an old dog hanging out with my family, also unnecessary in my opinion. Suddenly, Paolo erupts in anger over the trip to the village on account of puppies, and fires a question at the girl behind him: Tell me, Rachele, and forgive me for asking, why didn't your father have this dog fixed to spare himself and others all this trouble? Oh wait, do you even know what fixing means? Rachele knows. She has two friends with female dogs who will never give birth. Whereas her father thinks it's a sin to spay a purebred German hunting dog, even if she no longer is a hunting dog. What do you mean, purebred? To judge by her brother, who went out of his mind scratching the car door, there's no breeding here. Rachele silently considers this statement, digging her fingers in the dog's neck. Finally, she whispers: okay, it's not exactly her brother, he's just a pup she whelped a few years ago, who can't stop chasing after her.

Paolo laughs and speeds up. The rain ends. Rachele hugs the dog, lifts her right ear and blows into it gently to comfort her. The dog shakes her head, doesn't understand what Rachele wants from her. Maybe this time she won't have only two puppies, like last year, but more. At home a nice Israeli veterinarian named Yael takes care of her. She hasn't completed veterinary school, but Papà trusts her almost as much as he does the hospital director in Venice.

The dials on the English side are lit up, but no one is checking them. I was overly worried about the road this morning, Paolo confesses to his passenger, but Rachele doesn't hear him. Her head is pressed against the neck of her dog, who licks the girl's cheeks as she drifts into deep sleep, dreaming that the car isn't traveling on the flat open road, but is climbing a tall, steep hill, stubbornly, circuitously, straining and screeching, when suddenly she hears her father's voice, and the dog barking, jumping from the car, joyfully pouncing on her master, leaning her front paws on him, prancing around him. And drowsy Rachele enviously watches this outpouring of love from the dog. She loves him most of all, he's the most important to her. Me she licks, but him she kisses, and Mamma she ignores.

Riccardo pays Paolo, apparently adding a handsome holiday gift, since Paolo isn't complaining about the superfluous trip. But Rachele decides to complain, in his name as well. You sent us on an all-day boondoggle to Martina's village, Diana wasn't about to give birth, not there or on the road, or even soon. The whole way I was feeling her belly and didn't feel anything there. You worried for no reason, but if you were worried, Paolo could have brought her himself, he didn't need me. So instead of being with Nonno and Nonna who barely saw me, I was out there in the puddles and mud. And I didn't get to see my parrot. So tomorrow morning, first thing, no matter what, I want to go there. If I weren't so tired I'd run over to them now. No reason to run, Mamma says, the parrot escaped.

"The parrot escaped?" yells Rachele, "I warned you he might escape and you said why would he, and see, he did. What happened?"

"Nonna cleaned his cage and didn't notice the window was open, and all of a sudden he flew off and vanished."

"How stupid! Sorry, sorry, but why the big rush to clean the cage after one day?"

"It's okay, don't make it into a tragedy. The day after tomorrow Nonno will get you a new parrot."

"I don't want a new parrot, I wanted that parrot, only that one."

"What's the difference? Nonno will bring the same exact parrot."

"There is no such thing as the same exact parrot, so please, he shouldn't bring any parrot. I wanted only that parrot."

"But you barely saw him. You never really met him. What do you know about him?"

"That's exactly the point. Because I didn't get to know him, I want him all the more."

"But the cage is still there."

"I don't care, they can put anything they want in it, a snake."

17

Rachele takes a good look at Natalia Castellano, the teacher whose maternity leave has lasted longer than planned. Although she's ready to pick up the baton, the principal accompanies her at the first lesson, perhaps to caution the students to grant her the same attentiveness and good behavior accorded the newly retired teacher, currently warming herself in the Sicilian sunshine.

But when the principal leaves the room a mild commotion ensues. Hands fly up as several students ask to have their seats changed. Antonella, sitting in the back, insists on trading places with Rachele, who blocks her view of the teacher, "maybe because Rachele came back from Christmas even taller."

"I don't believe Rachele got taller during such a brief

holiday," the teacher remarks dryly, and asks Rachele to switch seats with Antonella.

Rachele is disappointed. If she sits in the rear of the class, it will be harder for the teacher to notice when she raises her hand to ask an intelligent question or give the right answer. So she suggests moving to the right, behind Andrea who sits near the door. If she must switch seats, better to move sideways than back.

As the teacher mulls the option of squeezing another desk and chair into the right-hand row, Andrea proves its feasibility by shoving his desk toward the door, making room behind him for a girl he's been in love with for over a year. Though he knows his acne and sad eyes will leave his love unrequited, he'll make do for now with the gentle words of thanks whispered behind him.

The teacher hands to the students worksheets she composed at home, to ease her return to the job and possibly get a bit of the rest her baby steals from her at night. Wait, is it a boy or a girl? Rachele raises her hand, Teacher, we, your students, are curious to know if your new baby is male or female.

"A baby boy," the teacher quickly replies, "an adorable baby but not easy."

Rachele wants to know his name.

"Antonio Castellano."

"A fine combination," confirms Rachele, and other students concur.

Now there's no avoiding the worksheets, which the teacher's husband, a future doctor, presumably helped her prepare, since they include a few math questions beyond the level of the class. The teacher agrees to drop them but nothing else in literature and grammar, history ancient and modern, geography and natural science, and even Church history. A broad range of questions, on which basis she seeks to learn how much her students know, what needs to be augmented, and what can be sacrificed.

During recess Rachele notices Andrea walking around her restlessly, as if her relocation directly behind him gives him special privileges or responsibilities. The next lesson is painting, always fun. The elderly art teacher, whose naïve paintings grace the school corridors, asks the students to paint an animal, imaginary or from memory. Rachele decides to paint the parrot that escaped, but before starting asks him how many colors, in his opinion, can be crowded into one parrot. I don't think there are more than five colors per parrot, says the teacher, but if it's an imaginary parrot, you can add two more. It's a semi-imaginary parrot, in reality I caught only a glimpse of him, explains Rachele. If that's the case, says the art teacher, don't overdo it, if you pile on too many colors, people won't know it's a parrot.

Painting is a disorderly class, with students trading brushes and tubes of paint, and forever running to the bathroom to refill jars with water. Rachele peeks over Andrea's shoulder to see what he's painting, but he's reluctant to reveal the dog he's trying to put on paper. I don't know if what came out looks like a dog at all.

"Why? You don't have your dog in mind?"

"We never had a dog, our house is too small for a dog. Maybe this'll be the neighbors' dog."

Rachele studies him. "Can I ask a personal question, a small one?"

"Sure, why not."

"Is your father still in the hospital?"

"My father?" Andrea recoils. "Why my father?"

"Our former teacher told me about him."

"Our former teacher? Who, Signora Gironi? Why?"

"Because my father will also go to a hospital soon."

"But the old lady got it mixed up," Andrea retorts irritably, "it's not my father who's sick, it's my mother, she's in the hospital."

"And your father?"

"Papà is fine, Papà is healthy, but why do you need to know?"

"Just to know."

"What's it to you?"

"Because our teacher said that now you're taking care of your brother."

"How does she know?"

"Why? It's not true?"

"It's true, but why is she telling you about my brother? Do you also have a brother you'll have to take care of?"

"No. I have no brothers or sisters."

"Then why?"

"To understand how you go to school and also take care of your brother."

"No problem, I just have to bring him to his nanny in the morning, and pick him up after school, then feed him and play with him, and if my father is late, to bathe him and put him to bed. That's all. But if you have no brother, why do you need to know?"

The teacher walks around for a look at the paintings. Your parrot's beak, he tells Rachele, needs to be bigger, its tongue is hiding in there.

"You're right, Professore," Rachele agrees, "I have to give him a bigger beak because he will be a parrot who speaks two languages."

"Which two languages?"

"Hebrew and Italian."

"Hebrew and Italian?" The teacher is amused. "And how will your parrot tell the difference between them?"

"He won't, the two languages are mixed together in his mind, so I'll enlarge not only his beak but his brain too."

Andrea's dog is a detailed portrait, all black with a white stripe around his neck, whereas the parrot is a colorful mishmash and she'll need to start over next time.

The day's last lesson begins, a music class that everyone likes, after which the students rush out. Rachele follows Andrea, who slows his pace to keep close to her.

"How come your parrot knows Hebrew?" He tries to connect before they part.

"He learned it from me. I'm studying Hebrew."

"You have a special school where they teach Hebrew?"

"In our synagogue there's a class taught by a rabbi, like your priest, only without a collar. He came to us from Israel, to teach us, a few girls, the Hebrew prayers, for our bat mitzvah, the celebration at age twelve."

"Bat mitzvah." Andrea tries out the Hebrew words. Rachele knows Andrea is in love with her. There are other boys in the class in love with her too. Indeed, Andrea is so excited by love that at one and the same time he wants to cling to her and also to run away. But this time she won't let him run away.

"You're going now to pick up your brother from the nanny?"

"That's right."

"Where does she live?"

"Not far, on Via Accademia."

"That's not very far. I can come with you."

"Why?"

"No reason. To see what your brother looks like."

"He looks a lot like me."

"But I bet also a little different. Would you mind? Maybe I'll have a brother like him someday."

"So come. But I can't take him from the nanny before three, you'll have to wait with me a while."

And since it's drizzling, they find shelter at a bus stop and wait there. Andrea can't believe his good fortune, the oddity of the rabbi who came from Israel notwithstanding. Other women and men arrive and wait as well, and when the church bells ring three o'clock they all head for the entrance of a nondescript apartment building and climb the stairs. What, asks Rachele, this nanny takes care of other children as well?

Toddlers in coats and caps emerge from the door of an ordinary flat. Here's my brother, says Andrea, his name is Alessandro. A boy in a black raincoat with a white collar runs toward them, and he really and truly resembles Andrea. And Rachele asks herself, am I crazy? What am I doing here? They go down the stairs and exit the building, but she needs to go east, and Andrea and his brother are headed in the opposite direction, so before they part, she asks Andrea if Alessandro will allow her to give him a kiss, just one.

Andrea blushes, he'd like the kiss for himself, but it's his brother Rachele wants to kiss, so he asks him: may my friend give you a kiss? And the little one squirms and whispers, why? But Rachele doesn't reply, she just leans over and plants a kiss on his cheek.

"That's all," she says, "one's enough for him."

18

Rabbi Yaakov Azoulay is spending Christmas and New Year's with his family in Jerusalem, not only to distance himself from the intensely Christian atmosphere of Italy during this season, but also to check on a new match. However, the suggested bride is not attractive enough to be worthy of such a notable Talmudic prodigy, and though he has not despaired of finding a mate in Israel, he has not given up hope of a match with a beautiful young Italian Jewess of means, who would return with him to Israel and be amused by the steadily growing nationalism in the Holy Land.

Therefore, the thirty-year-old rabbi agrees to extend his contract another year, through the year 2000, and continue his activities, which include holiday sermons, Hebrew lessons, and preparation for bar and bat mitzvahs for Jewish youngsters in four northern Italian cities: Mantua, Ferrara, Padua and Modena. Toward the end of January, the four Jewish girls, Rachele, Sabrina, Fiamma and Simonetta, are informed of the resumption of their lessons, under the auspices of the community but generously financed by the parents, who want to reinforce their daughters' Jewishness as a bulwark against intermarriage.

Rachele eagerly awaits the rabbi's return, because she loves Hebrew and misses the lofty language of the prayers, also because the rabbi has proven his talent and fortitude by dealing with questions that parents and other relatives avoid. Rachele's burning question has to do with the text of *Aleinu*, which she recited for Nonno Ernesto, who immediately grasped, as an intelligent gentile, the aggressive meaning of the Jewish prayer. And though out of love for his granddaughter he forgave the collective insult, he is still bitter about being forced to listen at the bat mitzvah service to a prayer hostile to his identity, even if spoken in a foreign tongue. Rachele is determined to find out, in this first lesson, whether it's possible to replace the *Aleinu* at the ceremony with something gentler and more human.

Adjoining the women's section of the little Tunisian synagogue on Via Corridoni is a modest library of religious books, and it is unclear whether it belongs to the women or is neutral territory that men too may freely enter. Rabbi Azoulay decided that a place whose walls bulge with sacred writings, yet lacking a *mehitzah* to segregate the sexes, is a proper venue for a man giving bat mitzvah lessons to girls in the Jewish community. He arrives there early to warm up the space with two electric heaters borrowed from the men's section so the warm air would compel the girls to shed coats and sweaters, remaining in lightweight blouses, in the sartorial spirit of the rabbis who wrote the marvelous texts two thousand years ago in the Mediterranean basin.

The four girls differ from one another in social status and religious stance. Sabrina is the daughter of middle-class Jewish parents who intend to immigrate to Israel upon completing their medical studies, thus their daughter's knowledge of Hebrew is important to them. Whereas Fiamma is the daughter of a Catholic woman of aristocratic lineage, who married a wealthy Jew but was forbidden by her parents to convert. So Fiamma is still not actually Jewish, but since her father wants her to celebrate her bat mitzvah with her Jewish friends, she stays after class for further study, preparation for conversion. Fiamma is dazzlingly beautiful, resembling her Catholic mother, and Rabbi Azoulay would prefer at least one other girl to be present in the private lesson, lest his being alone with the young beauty arouse indecent thoughts among those who enjoy indecent thoughts. The permanent participant in the conversion lessons is of course Rachele, thrilled by further study of Hebrew. In fact, Rachele is also a very pretty girl, but the tutorial conducted by an unmarried Israeli rabbi with two beautiful girls ought not arouse erotic suspicions even if it looks peculiar.

Today, at the beginning of the lesson, before discussing theological questions with his pupils, or the halakhic and moral significance of age twelve and the view of the ancient rabbis that girls of twelve are wiser than boys of twelve, Rabbi Azoulay turns to mundane matters, asking them to describe, in Hebrew, important experiences in their lives since last they met, more than a month ago. The girls' Hebrew is halting, but the rabbi's Italian is also substandard, so the two languages complement one another, sometimes with surprise or embarrassment, other times with merry laughter. And when the negotiation of Hebrew and Italian is done, the moment comes to open the *siddurim* to practice the words and melodies of the blessings for the ceremonies in the spring. But this time Rachele interrupts the lesson, and in garbled Hebrew, assisted here and there by Italian, talks about a beloved Grandpa, who without understanding the holy tongue intuited the offense and hostility hidden in the Jewish prayer, and with the brazenness of an only granddaughter in a privileged family, she demands that the rabbi find a different prayer, which even if it praises and extols the Jews, doesn't insult someone who wasn't lucky enough to be one of them.

The rabbi is astonished by the aggressiveness of a young student who takes an ancient prayer literally. And instead of dismissing her with some worn-out rabbinic adage, he leafs through the prayerbook, but with his eyes closed, as if trying to locate, by touch, a milder text that would not discomfit Jews whose families include goyim. The four girls gaze at the rabbi, who after long silence pulls from the shelf a volume of Psalms, and with the confidence of a true scholar he replaces *Aleinu l'shabeah* with a supplication that anyone may address to his God without excluding others.

A Psalm of David. How long, O Lord, will you ignore me forever? How long will you hide your face from me? How long shall I take counsel in my soul, having sorrow in my heart all day? How long shall my enemy be exalted over me? Behold, and answer me, O Lord my God, lighten my eyes, lest I sleep the sleep of death, lest mine enemy say: "I have prevailed against him," lest my adversaries rejoice when I fall. And as for me, in your kindness do I trust; my heart shall rejoice in your salvation. I will sing unto the Lord, for he has been good to me.

And he passes the open book to the four girls, who huddle together and read the short psalm, and even if unfamiliar with most of the words, are ready to adopt it as a substitute for the racist prayer.

But the lesson does not conclude with a hymn from holy writ but with a simple Israeli song the rabbi sings, waving his hands. The Israeli tune pleases the girls more than sacred songs, and they join in, waving as they sing, and the melody helps them understand the words:

> Sometimes I'm sad
> And sometimes I'm glad.
> Sometimes I recall
> And sometimes forget.
> Sometimes I'm full,
> Sometimes hungry.
> Sometimes I'm angry
> And sometimes loving.
> But I always stay me.
> I always stay me.
> Always stay me!

Sometimes I'm big
And sometimes small.
Sometimes I'm a hero
Sometimes a coward
Sometimes together
Sometimes alone
Sometimes in the middle
Sometimes on the side.
But I always stay me.
I always stay me.
Always stay me!

Sometimes I'm a violin
Sometimes a set of drums
Sometimes I'm a summer's day
And sometimes snow and sleet.
Sometimes I'm lazy
And sometimes work hard.
Sometimes I'm sweet
And sometimes sour.
But I always stay me.
Always stay me.
Always stay me!

Sometimes I'm stupid
Sometimes I'm smart.
Sometimes I'm first

And sometimes third.
Sometimes I catch
Sometimes I get caught.
Sometimes I'm huge
And sometimes just a tot.
But I always stay me.
Always stay me.
Always stay me!

The lesson ends in high spirits. Sabrina and Simonetta, wearing their coats and scarves, say goodbye to Fiamma, whose Jewishness remains incomplete. Tell me, says the rabbi to Rachele, the auditor of Fiamma's lessons, is what I heard in the community true, that two weeks from now you're moving to Venice? To live there? No. We'll just be staying with Grandma when Papà is in the hospital, a famous Turkish surgeon who comes here every year for Carnival will perform the operation.

"When does Carnival begin?"

"Next week."

"In the three years I've served the Jews of northern Italy, I've never been to this Carnival, and this is my last year here."

"Your last year?" Fiamma whispers sadly.

"Yes, so you must complete your conversion before I leave for Israel."

"She'll do it," Rachele promises for her. "What will you teach her today?"

"Maybe let's review the laws of kosher food."

"Very good," confirms Rachele, the self-appointed manager of Fiamma, "I also get confused about how long you have to wait between milk and meat, how long after cheese can you eat meat, how long to wait for cheese after meat. Therefore, Rabbi, could you write it all down in an orderly fashion, because Fiamma's mother, who will never be Jewish, can't understand on her own the logic of this waiting, and a page in your handwriting would help. If you're worried about mistakes in Italian, we can fix them for you."

Rabbi Azoulay smiles warmly. If Rachele were ten years older, he would consider enlisting a matchmaker, and if he were ten years younger, he'd be willing to wait ten years until she came of age. But in ten more years he'll be forty, and even ten more years at the elite Porat Yosef yeshiva would not qualify him to join a family of lawyers. His curiosity therefore shifts to the Venice Carnival. Perhaps his fortunes would take a good turn there. And the two of you, he asks his students, have you been to this Carnival? If so, tell me a little about it.

"They took me there once," says Fiamma, "but during the day, because at night it's only for grownups."

"My Grandma let me have a peek at night," says Rachele, "but one mask started chasing me, so I went home."

"Why Grandma?"

"I already told you, she lives in Venice. And you, Rabbi, if you want to wander around there at night, you could sleep at her house, it's enormous."

"But what happens at the Carnival?"

"People wear disguises."

"Do you have to?"

"You don't have to, it's just fun, that's the main thing, the masquerade, and there are costumes that are completely insane."

"Not just insane," adds Fiamma, "also scary, truly scary."

"But the whole thing is a show, nothing is real. And if you walk into a church and think they're praying, you should know it's not prayers, it's a show. And a show can't also be a prayer service."

The rabbi gazes warmly at his favorite student, but like her old teacher, he too hedges his answer. Prayer or play, it all depends on the actor.

19

The Venetian grandmother is pleased to comply with Rachele's request to house Rabbi Azoulay, but frankly baffled that he chose Carnival to acquaint himself with the culture and history of Venice. She plans to give him the room where Rachele always stays, with the big bed in which tender newborns would sleep at the bosoms of their mothers. Rabbi Yaakov Azoulay is of Tunisian ancestry, able to chat with his many relatives in colonial French, one of the many languages spoken fluently by the Grandma, auguring the likelihood of a fruitful encounter.

Rachele asks Paolo to order a gondola for the rabbi at the train station but forgets to warn the guest that the gondolier will probably be deaf and mute. But Yaakov Azoulay is unfazed by the muteness as he glides down the

Grand Canal. During his yeshiva days, his Talmud study partners included a deaf and mute partner, who proved to be sharp and perceptive.

The rabbi arrives in late afternoon, and is immediately invited to a meal of cheeses, vegetables, and fruit, served only with toast, for fear of the pig fat. Why the obsession of Jews with pigs? The grandmother interrogates the guest in French. First of all, it's not only a Jewish obsession, smiles the rabbi defensively, the Muslims also loathe the pig, and they constitute half of the world's monotheists. Besides, the pig is an ugly creature, its nose especially. But Grandma impishly conjectures the pig may feel important that so many monotheists are wary of it. Let him think what he wants, Signora Luzzatto, answers the rabbi, we're not interested in what the pig feels but what God thinks of him.

"Nice," the grandmother acknowledges the sensible answer. "In any case, Rachele told me she promised you she'd keep kosher until her bat mitzvah."

"And I hope she sticks with it after I leave. She's a charming and intelligent girl, and I'll let you in on a strange secret, but don't get angry, Signora, says the rabbi, turning beet-red, his voice quavering. If I had the patience I would extend my bachelorhood another ten years and return to Italy and approach her through a matchmaker."

"I sincerely hope you won't have the patience," smiles the Grandma. "How old are you now, Rabbi?"

"Thirty-one."

"In which case, I'm sure your parents lost patience a long time ago."

"Apparently so," sighs the rabbi.

"Besides which, you'd surely take her to Israel. So please save your patience for someone who already lives there. Rachele is my only grandchild. And I won't let her disappear on me, not even to the Holy Land, which has too many Jews in any case. Some Jews should be preserved in Italy too, otherwise the Italians will forget we exist. But you didn't come tonight for matchmaking, so first of all, here's the address of my house, so you can find it when you come back at night."

"Perhaps also a key, so I won't wake anybody?"

"No need. I'm a very light sleeper, and if you ring the bell, I or one of the servants will open the door. Another thing, how much money are you carrying with you?"

"Around three hundred euros."

"Too much. Leave two hundred here and take only a hundred. During Carnival there are pickpockets roaming around, with and without costumes, all of them incredibly quick. And don't you walk around as you are, people will think you're an Italian masquerading as a rabbi. Buy yourself a mask."

"A mask?"

"Yes, a mask. This is Carnival."

"And where does one buy masks?"

"Everywhere. It needn't be big, just something that covers the eyes and nose, a bigger mask might interfere with your walking, you could trip and, heaven forbid, fall into a canal."

"God save us. And where should I go? Where's the heart of the Carnival?"

"In Piazza San Marco, go into the cathedral. Don't worry, there are no prayers during Carnival, just funny shows."

"Fine, I'll take my life in my hands, I'll have something to tell friends in Israel, provided I come back here safely. Your home, Signora Luzzatto, is simply gorgeous."

"I'd be delighted, Rabbi Azoulay, to host you here for more than one night, and maybe you would teach me things I never knew about the Jews, but the day after tomorrow my son Riccardo, Rachele's father, is coming to get ready for his surgery."

"Yes, Rachele told me about a genius brain surgeon from Turkey who comes every year to Carnival."

"She also managed to tell you about this surgeon? She doesn't miss a thing. It's no accident that her grandfather, my former husband, pins her compositions to his office wall."

"The lawyer?"

"Her father is also a lawyer."

"And she'll of course want to be a lawyer. In Israel every third person is a lawyer."

"No, she won't be a lawyer. She wants to be a judge."

"Who's she going to judge?"

"All of us."

And she hands the rabbi a map of Venice, with her house circled. You cross the Grand Canal on the Accademia Bridge, and anyone you ask can tell you how to get from there to Piazza San Marco.

And Rabbi Azoulay fumbles his way through the narrow alleys, crossing bridges beneath the night sky, the stars extinguished by searchlights and fireworks. Trailing costumed revelers, he comes upon a row of stalls where masks are sold, moving from stall to stall until one strikes his fancy, offering a selection of black robes and white priestly collars. Rabbi Azoulay has always regretted that rabbis did not have something like the collars that priests wear even with business suits, something to indicate that they are rabbis, without embellishing themselves with words of Torah.

He buys a collar and asks the seller to help him put it on, she offers him a robe too. Really, why not? says the rabbi to himself. In Italy, better a rabbi dressed up like a priest than a priest dressed like a rabbi. Besides, the robe costs only thirty-five euros, and though it's made of thin, cheap cloth, it warms the body on this cold night. If I just add a mask to hide my short sidelocks, the rabbi convinces himself, I could fit right into this Carnival masquerade with no danger that some Jew at whose synagogue I deliver holiday sermons will recognize me.

But he asks the seller to undo the crucifix embroidered on the back of the robe. The fabric is thin, she says, and if I start undoing it, I might make holes. We see a lot of embroidered crosses at Carnival, nobody will think you're a priest, especially if you put on a mask and keep wearing your hat.

Without delay Azoulay enters the basilica, tagging along with a group of dignitaries led by a man wrapped in an Italian flag, flanked by a police captain with a black sword. A tall, thin man towers over the group, wearing a Turkish fez and chattering in English.

Maybe he's the Turkish surgeon, thinks Azoulay, following him with excitement toward a chapel, to the accompaniment of a marching band. This is not the first time he has ventured deep into a church, but when he removes his hat, his kippah sits squarely on his head, so he

can broaden his education and satisfy his curiosity without violating his faith.

Suddenly two men dressed in black, belted with sashes,
squeeze into the chapel, tall furry *shtreimels* on their heads,
with sidelocks, absurdly long, surreal, impossible, dangling
from underneath, two young men dressed up as Hasidim,
but are they only Italian, or Jewish as well?

The pair gleefully approach Azoulay, maybe craving inter-
faith dialogue, and the rabbi is taken aback and retreats
toward the exit, making his way among clowns and acro-
bats, but the two Hasidim follow him closely, not ceding
an inch. Are these Jews masquerading as ultra-Orthodox?
Why do they insist on following him? Maybe these are
Jews who hear his sermons, who recognized him despite
the robe and the cross? Could a goy dress up, with such
meticulous attention to detail, like a *haredi*? Where do
they sell *shtreimels* like these around here? For a moment,
he wants to strip off the robe and crucifix but is afraid
to reveal himself as a mere rabbi. Where's the Accademia
bridge? He urgently asks passersby, strange creatures,
kings and princesses, animals and mythological winged
beasts, where's the Accademia bridge, where does one
cross the Grand Canal? And they all show him the way,
everyone knows the way. He runs and the moon wobbles

above him. The Grandma's house is all lit up. He rings the doorbell uneasily.

Not a servant but the Grandma opens the door, statuesque in a strange, breathtaking nightgown, perhaps a royal gown from the time of the Renaissance. Back so soon, Rabbi Azoulay?

"Yes," he replies, swiftly removing his robe and undoing the collar, "I am a quiet Jerusalemite, and in Jerusalem we have only simple Jews and Arabs, and here frightening creatures are wandering around. But I think, Signora Luzzatto, that I recognized the Turkish surgeon who has come to save your son."

"You're mistaken, the Turkish surgeon postponed his arrival, and who knows if he'll get here at all." A broken sob bursts from deep within her, the sobbing of a person who seldom cries.

"Why despair, madame," he approaches her hesitantly, "if not him, another surgeon will do it, and I will assist him with prayers. From the moment he is anaesthetized on the operating table, until he wakes up, with God's help, I will bind him to us with the poetry of Psalms, so he won't be tempted to escape to the world of the spirits. I'll read the whole book, over and over, just tell me when to begin."

20

Prior to hospitalization and surgery, Papà and Mamma go to Venice to stay with the grandmother, and Rachele moves to Grandpa Sergio's house, farther from her school than Nonno Ernesto and Nonna Paula's, but a big house, with servants to help look after the young guest.

A taxi takes Rachele to school every morning, and brings her back at the end of the day. But since the student is embarrassed to arrive in a taxi, she asks the driver to stop two blocks away and she continues on foot, sometimes wet and shivering from the rain. The young teacher is a disappointment. She poses questions only rarely to her students, and doesn't expect intelligent answers. Rachele

realizes there's no point in sitting close to the front, behind Andrea, where a raised hand can get attention, because the need to do so is rare. On rainy days the side aisle
is crammed with raincoats, umbrellas, and galoshes, and
though Andrea tries to make room for his beloved behind
him, Rachele resigns herself and moves to the place in the
rear vacated by Antonella. Instead of making an effort to
display her intelligence, she stares out the window at the
world, while the teacher drowses at her desk.

The young teacher is truly exhausted, and takes every opportunity to hand out worksheets for students to tackle
independently while she grabs forty winks. In the morning hours her baby is cared for by an older woman, whose
long experience enables her to lull him into deep slumber,
so from early evening and into the night, the boy wants
to play with his mother and refuses to go to sleep. His father, a fourth-year medical student, has taken on a night
shift at the Red Cross clinic to pay for his studies and his
share of the mortgage. To his credit, while on night duty
he doesn't forget his wife struggling with their infant son.
He prepares the worksheets that his wife distributes to
her students and collects after the lesson, which she then
gives back to him for grading. But he writes his comments
and the grade in a note to his wife, who will copy them

out in her handwriting, to show her devotion to the students and their parents.

Grandpa Sergio travels every two days to the hospital in Venice to visit his son, and brings warm greetings to Rachele. He doesn't describe the medical tests in detail, nor does he say when, and if, the surgeon will arrive. When the daughter talks on the phone with her father or mother, she fears asking questions whose answers will heighten her anxiety.

Then the day comes when not only Grandpa Sergio and his wife travel to the hospital, but also Nonno Ernesto and Nonna Paula, and Rachele senses that something is happening. It's a wintry day, without rain. Through the classroom window she sees that the schoolyard is empty. One lone boy from an upper grade, wearing a pilot's cap, shoots a basketball incessantly at the hoop, with no success. The ball keeps hitting the rim, producing a metallic thud, and bounces to the edge of the court. But the boy doesn't give up, he chases the ball, tries again, and again misses.

The pilot's cap hides his face, but at one point the wind carries off the cap and his identity is revealed. It's Enrico, the handsome lad who brought her to the principal on the day before Christmas. Enrico, whom the old teacher dubbed Cicillo, the boy in the story who cared for the man he thought was his father. Enrico, whom I fell in love with when he led me down the empty corridor, and I looked for in the snow of the Dolomites. She gets up, lays the worksheet on the teacher's desk, and without asking permission, and with no coat, only a light sweater, heads to the schoolyard.

"You're Enrico." She touches his sleeve. "Remember me? Rachele Luzzatto, you took me to the principal."

Enrico looks at her closely, of course he remembers her, the girl whose father wouldn't let her be the Mother of God in the play, because he's a Jew.

"I'm a Jew too, same as he," she says, as if revealing a secret. "I've been watching you for a long time from the classroom window, and I'm surprised you've never managed to get the ball in the basket."

"On purpose," he shouts. "I miss on purpose, I hit the rim on purpose."

"On purpose?"

"Yes, on purpose."

"Why?"

"Because I'm angry at the world."

"Which world?"

"The whole world. Everything." And he hurls the ball at the basket, and in his excitement he fails to fail, and the ball falls through the net and out the bottom.

"You see," he smiles, "you confused me." And Rachele returns the smile.

"I went to see our old teacher Emilia Gironi and I even slept over at her house, and she mentioned you and said your mother has been in the hospital a long time."

"My mother? Not so," he says, blushing. "She got confused, or else you're confused. My father was in the hospital. Maybe that's why she called me Cicillo."

"Your father, not your mother? What happened to him?"

"He's gone."

"Your father?"

"My father."

Rachele trembles, can barely stand on her feet. Enrico's heart goes out to the pretty girl shivering in a flimsy sweater.

"Gone when?"

"Two days after the holiday."

"Which holiday?"

"Christmas?"

"And your mother?"

"My mother is fine. She's not sick."

"Do you have a brother or sister?"

"I have two older sisters. One has a baby. Why do you ask?"

Rachele's eyes are closed, she hugs herself with both arms. She's cold.

"Why'd you go out like that without a coat," says Enrico, who takes off his jacket and helps her put it on.

"My father is also in the hospital."

"The father who wouldn't let you play the Mother of God."

"Same father."

21

Since, as it turns out, the exalted Turkish surgeon is not coming to Venice this year, the hospital director must rely on two Italian doctors for the complicated operation, which he himself supervises. Although there's no way to tell whether the excised "appendage" has left hidden traces, it would seem the surgery has achieved its goal. Family members, as well as the family physician, who anxiously awaited the patient's full return to consciousness to confirm that his mental acuity and sense of humor were unimpaired, are pleased to find Riccardo recovering nicely. And indeed after just a few days he is granted permission to continue his recuperation at his mother's house, not far from the hospital.

✳ ✳ ✳

The time has come for the only child, prevented till now from visiting her father, to be allowed to do so. Grandpa informs the school principal, who gives her approval. But before the grandfather and granddaughter depart for Venice, they make a detour to the district court, where Sergio stands in for his son at the closing arguments of a case that can no longer be postponed.

This is not Rachele's first visit to a courtroom. From time to time, during school vacations, her father would take her along, so that she would be impressed by his work and his colleagues would be impressed by her. There are people here who recognize the girl and ask about her father. Tell him his friends hope to see him back here soon, they say, and she accepts the assignment, but to do so properly, she needs everyone to write their names on a piece of paper.

Waiting in the courtroom are the public prosecutor and the defendant, an Albanian immigrant of about forty-five, who entered Italy illegally five years ago. To become a citizen, he married a young Italian woman, who bore him a son, but he did not disclose the fact that he was already married with children, whom he left behind in his homeland.

When the judge enters the courtroom, all rise in her honor, but before sitting down she approaches Sergio

Luzzatto to inquire about his son. The grandfather introduces Rachele and informs the judge that they are about to go to Venice to visit the patient. In that case, she says to the girl, give your father my regards, and Rachele asks her to add her name to the piece of paper. The girl's assertiveness amuses the judge, who writes down her name and title, and wants to know if Rachele is planning to be a lawyer, like her Grandpa and father.

"Not a lawyer, someone like you."

"Meaning?"

"A judge."

"And whom would you like to judge?"

"Anyone who needs justice."

At the hearing Sergio Luzzatto seems confused, as if unprepared for the prosecutor's argument. A case like this is unfamiliar to a lawyer specializing in real estate. Her father deals mainly with torts and contracts, but if he took this case, it was obviously important to him for a reason, and he would have defended the Albanian better than his father. Rachele is aware that the judge, who was so nice to her, shows little mercy toward the Albanian's Italian wife, who sits silently in the courtroom, her arm around the little boy beside her.

On the train to Venice, Rachele can't help thinking about the defendant's face, so handsome and so sad. No doubt his good looks enabled him to land such a young wife, and have a child, who will now grow up in Italy without a father. The Luzzattos are a wealthy family, and Rachele playfully imagines an impossible scenario wherein her family volunteers to raise the boy, who being a bit Muslim and a bit Christian would be a bit Jewish too.

Rachele hasn't seen her father for more than two weeks, and she's shocked when they meet, because Nonno Ernesto hadn't told her that her father's head was shaved for surgery. But that morning Grandma told her she had to be strong, even if Papà looks strange to her, or even different. Remember, she said, it is the same father who loves you infinitely.

22

The room she enters bears no resemblance to the lovely room where she stayed when she returned from the Dolomites. Now it's full of stuff, some of which arrived from the hospital with the patient. Papà lies on his side, napping. His newly bald head, by now unbandaged, gleams above the blanket. Rachele trembles, hesitates, and leans first toward the dog, also lying on her side, nursing her one new pup. The dog wags her tail, but growls to warn her mistress not to touch the newborn.

"This year we had only one," she says to her father, who hasn't yet turned to face her, "so who will we give it to?"

"Nobody. For now you'll take care of it."

"He doesn't look anything like Diana, he's a different breed."

"Nowadays the breeds are blended. Even horses. Come here, Rachele, come closer."

He feels under the blanket and pulls out the partisan's beret the principal gave her before Christmas, putting it on his head.

"See, now I'm also a partisan."

"Who are the partisans?"

"The ones who confused and surprised the enemy. Now I'll confuse the enemy, the one that invaded my head."

Rachele wants to say something, but the sentence is stuck in her throat. She sits on the old hospital birthing bed and lies down beside her father to cheer him up. Riccardo reaches out and touches her.

"My baby girl is back . . ."

"You'll leave me all alone . . ."

"Why alone? You have everyone here around you."

"Everyone? Everyone's gone. You know that without you I have no one. Without you I'll have to go look for the Holy Spirit, the one you wouldn't let hug me in the play."

Where will you look for it?"

"In the world."

"Which world?"

"I'll ask the teacher, the rabbi . . . Maybe I'll look for it in the place where this baby of theirs was born, maybe in Jerusalem, where Sabrina will live when her parents are doctors."

"There is no Holy Spirit in Jerusalem. Nor anywhere else."

"So who was that baby's father?"

"Maybe they called him the Holy Spirit, but just an ordinary wind blew there, a wind like other winds."

"If so, I'll find it among the winds and remind it to be a Holy Spirit. Come back and be a Holy Spirit, I will command it, beg it, convince it."

"It can't be, because it never was. That's why I didn't want you to play the Mother of God, so you wouldn't believe there was once a Holy Spirit, which might come back and bring another God into the world."

"No, not another God, you're right, Papà, the world doesn't need another God, there are too many already."

"So what should be born to you?"

"Not *to* me, *with* me."

"With you?"

"Yes, with me. Not a God but a brother, simply a brother, a brother to be with me when you are gone."

Here ends A. B. Yehoshua's
The Only Daughter.

The first edition of the book was printed and
bound at Lakeside Book Company
in Harrisonburg, Virginia, March 2023.

A NOTE ON THE TYPE

The text of this novel was set in Garamond Premier, a typeface designed by Robert Slimbach over the course of ten years. Released in 2005, its seeds were planted during Slimbach's development of the Adobe Garamond font family, also based in the work of Claude Garamond (1499–1561) and Robert Granjon (1513–1590). In 1994, a visit to Antwerp, Belgium, served as the catalyst for Slimbach's second interpretation. Garamond Premier differentiates itself from other revivals through its direct basis on the hand-cut models Slimbach studied, faithfully recapturing the elevated grace and clarity of its precursor.

HarperVia

An imprint dedicated to publishing international voices,
offering readers a chance to encounter other lives and
other points of view via the language of the imagination.